Rue
Reminiscence of the lost

Naseha Sameen

Ukiyoto Publishing

All global publishing rights are held by

Ukiyoto Publishing

Published in 2023

Content Copyright © Naseha Sameen

ISBN 9789360165987

*All rights reserved.
No part of this publication may be reproduced, transmitted, or stored in a retrieval system, in any form by any means, electronic, mechanical, photocopying, recording or otherwise, without the prior permission of the publisher.*

The moral rights of the author have been asserted.

This is a work of fiction. Names, characters, businesses, places, events, locales, and incidents are either the products of the author's imagination or used in a fictitious manner. Any resemblance to actual persons, living or dead, or actual events is purely coincidental.

This book is sold subject to the condition that it shall not by way of trade or otherwise, be lent, resold, hired out or otherwise circulated, without the publisher's prior consent, in any form of binding or cover other than that in which it is published.

Dedication

To the dreamer who realized an impossible love
Cover Design: K. S. Alok Ranjan

Contents

Part – I: The Body And The Burden Of Truth	**1**
Wake-Up Call	2
Passion Inherited	11
The Court Case	22
Motive & Intent	30
A Lead	45
An Arrest	55
The Challenge	63
The Hearing	73
The Judgement	81
Part – II: Transcended & Home Truth	**91**
Hello C	92
Growing Up	106
A Friend	117
In Love	129
A Proposal	135
Part – III: Their Versions Of Truth	**142**
Proclivity	143
Obsession	146
Anger	152
Respite	157
Indignation	164
Helpless	173
Invidious	179
Despair	184
Part – Iv: Truth, Nothing But The Truth	**190**
An Announcement	191

A Realization	197
A Transformation	202
An Understanding	208
An Inadvertence	214
A Damnation	218

Characters — 227

About the Author — *238*

Part – I: The Body And The Burden Of Truth

Wake-Up Call

Heavy fog had enveloped the long stretch of Sohna Road. It was 4:00 am, and yet it was dark. Visibility was less than 1 foot ahead. A dim streak of light from streetlamps was fighting a lost war. They were lost in the sea of smaze cloaking the vast stretch of land on either side of the road, which the real estate moguls had brought but were still to develop, waiting for the right economy. Orange balls of faint fire were floating on the muddled air of fresh grass, sleepy red soil, and a faint smell of petroleum. It has been this foggy since the past two weeks. People of Gurugram had love and hate relationship with fog. They love it from the comfort of their homes but driving through fog in 2°C[1]. All the turnings looked alike, no landmarks visible, no street name or familiar houses to spot on. The world that was home a few hours ago was alien now. Everything looked surreal. A page out of Death's diary when everything had forgotten to breathe. At that ungodly hour, nobody in their right mind would venture out. It was the hour for daredevils or romantic hearts to venture out to either conquer the haze or get lost. Fewer bikes and cars were crawling with their taillights on. Bijlee was neither a daredevil nor a romantic heart. If she could avoid it, she would have. Abhishikta was not answering her phone. She was supposed to start for Indira Gandhi International Airport. The flight's

---

[1] *2°C or Celsius is equivalent to 35.6°F.*

departure time was at 9:00am. She had asked her aunt Bijlee to give her a wake-up call at 4:00am. Abhishikta wanted to say goodbye to her and the rest of the family before hitting the road at 5:00am. She would still have time to take a slight detour from IFFCO chowk to Maruti Udyog to have one final time the nukkad-wali chai.[2] before flying.

A sense of foreboding gripped Bijlee as the car raced towards Abhishikta's farmhouse from their villa on Golf Course Road. She looked at her brother Dr. Divyansh with irritation. He was dozing off. He had accompanied her so that she would just shut up. Bijlee loved nothing more than theorizing the worst-case scenario for everything in life. Yet, he did not feel anything was amiss. Divyansh knew how much his sister thrived on such negativities.

There was uneasy calmness that reflected through the windows. Did Abhishikta leave without saying goodbye? Why was her mobile switched off? The windows were ajar. There was feeble light and a faint sound of music floating from the bedroom window. Dr. Divyansh was immediately alert. He dug into his pocket to fish out the keys, but it was not required. The door was unlocked. Warily they entered the house calling out her name.

"Abby, Abby, are you there?"

"Abby, is everything okay? Abby, are you home?"

---

[2] *Vendor selling tea on the corner of the street. Their business starts pretty early, at 3:00 am, when they start boiling tea leaves in milk with sugar and small cardamom for an hour to serve to the customers who would come in for the first shift at 4:00 am.*

One after another, they switched the lights in the room they entered. Watchfully they entered the bedroom where the lights were on. There Abby was! Sleeping! Bijlee lumbered towards the bed, apprehensive. Dr. Divyansh held her to stop her. Abby was not to be disturbed. She was sleeping peacefully. Sleeping on her bed. She couldn't hear them call out. She was in deep eternal sleep of death.

Silently the brother and the sister moved out from the room. Switching off the lights. Bijlee was cowered in the corner of the settee, looking dazed. Her petite stature of 4 ½ feet with short hair colored pitch black in a delicate cotton saree looked like a disfigured football. Her brother Dr. Divyansh was pacing up and down, making some calls.

Every ten minutes Bijlee would wail, "Divyansh, why can't we call a doctor. Who knows, she is just in a coma? We will be in trouble if she dies."

Impatiently, Dr. Divyansh would reply the identical explanation again and again, "I am a doctor, and I know nothing can be done now. She is gone. Dead! Dead as a doornail. Like it or not. We are in trouble. But before I call the authorities and make this public. I must understand what happened here and how much trouble we are in."

"Are you trying to dispose of the body?"

"Hell No! Bijlee, Have you lost it. We need to understand what went down here and gather all information before making that call. Can you just shut up till I do that?"

Dr. Divyansh's next call was to Irina, Abby's personal assistant.

Irina was not expecting any call at 5:45 am in the morning. Trying not to open her eyes, she replied. The next second, she was wide awake. Her place in sector 56 was barely 10 mins drive. Reachability was one of the factors Abby considered while hiring her. And she was never disappointed. Irina could directly reach all places from where Abby needed her in under 40 mins except one.

Dr. Divyansh slumped on another settee. Unlike Bijlee, who had taken care to change to a saree, comb her hair and apply basic make-up before starting, Dr. Divyansh had thrown his dressing gown over his pajamas. He cared not to brush his tangled hair, and he looked like a mess. He had made a some calls. Before he called the cops, he needed to catch his breath.

The first to come in the hall was the caretaker. He was closest, sleeping in in the servant's quarters. He stood, trying to avert his bloodshot eyes. His breath reeked of some cheap liquor and puke. He was standing behind Divyansh.

Irina reached in 10 mins. She was trembling. Divyansh gave her a glass of red wine to calm her nerves. They were now waiting for the cops to arrive.

---

15 km from there in Palam Vihar, inspector Jai Prakash Chautala was sleeping peacefully when constable Hari Krishna called. The death of the owner of six theme

restaurants would bring in some amount of scrutiny. So, he needed to wake up Jai.

In a sleepy voice, Jai asked, "Who died, Hari, that you had to call me? Is a man not entitled to to sleep?"

"Sir, the owner of Cena Cosmica, Abhishikta Vats, is dead. Please rush to her farmhouse on Sohna Road. Her uncle Dr. Divyansh called."

Jai woke up in a jiffy. Barely he had an hour or two of sleep. Previous night he had accompanied the patrol team to various malls. 31st Dec night increases the incidents of drunken driving and eve teasing. Jai reached home around 3:00 am. He switched off his TV that was still playing "NCIS"[3]. and started getting ready.

Abby's aunt Bijlee, Dr. Divyansh, and Irina were sitting. The caretaker of the farm was standing behind Dr. Divyansh's chair. Inspector Jai was taken to Abby as soon as he arrived. Medical Examiner was still on the way.

A draught of cold air greeted the team as they entered.

"Who would switch on the AC in NCR[4]'s winter?" wondered Jai as the lights were switched on in the room. "Did any of you switch on the AC?" he inquired.

AC in winter. Effective means to keep the body fresh.

Aunt Bijlee, Dr. Divyansh, the caretaker, and Irina nodded to confirm a "No".

---

[3] *NCIS - American police procedural television series.*
[4] *NCR – Near Capital Region – Basically encompasses Delhi, Gurugram, and Noida.*

Abby was on the bed. Jai's eyes scanned every inch of the room. Nothing seemed to be out of place. Then, putting on his gloves, he moved towards Abby. Her body was pale, but rigor mortis had not set in. Abby was in a red dress; red stilettos were prudently placed on one side of the bed. Her hands folded just under her breast. Studs of diamond were in her ears, and a simple solitaire in a plain chain was on her neck. Music was still on; the system was on a wooden cabinet above the bed. Above it was another cabinet filled with books.

"So, Ms. Abhishikta loved thriller novels," exclaimed Jai as he picked up a half-read novel, "The Captive[5]," from her side table."

Jai inspected the adjoining corridor, kitchen and dining space, and guest bathroom connected to her room. Everything was arranged in place. No signs of any struggle, though the front door not being locked raised doubts. Medical Examiner with crime scene expert arrived. Processing the body and crime scene commenced as Jai followed the group to the hall to get some answers.

Suicides are generally behind locked doors. No struggles. Did Abhishikta trust the perpetrator? Did she let the perp in? Perp could be someone known to her.

Jai took out his notebook to start his routine investigation, "I am aware Ms. Abhishikta has theme restaurants. Is there anything else she was involved in?"

---

5 The Captive: Psychological Thriller by Lavanya Nukavarapu. The story is how multiple lives become entangled when a kidnapped girl escapes and sets the alarms ringing on at least 15 unsolved murder cases, primarily involving female victims.

Irina was the first to answer, "AV, I mean Abhishikta's world revolved around her theme restaurants. When she inherited the business, it was just restaurants in sector 56 and in United Cyber Park. She put a soul in these and converted them to Space Theme Restaurants, 'Cena Cosmica'. Soon, she opened branches in Mall Road, in Gold Souk, in Leisure Valley, and in Ambience Mall. She was that good. Her life revolved around her work." Irina's voice had a sense of pride as she recalled AV's accomplishments.

"Were there any threatening calls made to the deceased?" They looked at around and replied negatively. They had no such information.

"Dr. Divyansh and Bijlee ma'am, was your niece involved with anybody…romantically?"

Dr. Divyansh replied quickly, "She loved her work."

"Did AV have any enemies?"

Irina added, "In the business world, she had scores of rivals, but I don't think she had any enemies. She had no enemies."

A new voice added, "Whole world was her enemy, and she was the identical to the world. She hated everybody". A drunken young man in his twenties, with an unkempt appearance came in. Seems he had been drinking the whole night.

"Inspector, want to know about her enemies? See around yourself, each one of us, me …" before he could complete his sentence, Dr. Divyansh stopped him. Color faded from his face when he saw Shay, his son, standing at the hall's entrance, drunk and spiteful. He hurried and took Shay away on the pretext of him being too drunk to talk any sense.

Bijlee kept adding a small wail, "Oh, my pet, my girl, why did you leave us alone!" after each of her answers. If she was acting, it was terrible. Irina was sad but tried to sound as professional as possible. Dr. Divyansh seemed normal till his son showed up. After that, he was shaky when he returned to the hall.

The specialists were bagging and tagging the pieces of evidence. Assistant ME was accompanying AV's body to the autopsy. Jai's work here seemed to be done for today.

From the first interview, Jai could sum up

Cause: Murder or suicide – not yet confirmed.

People close: Aunt - Bijlee, Uncle – Dr. Divyansh, Cousin - Shay, Personal Assistant – Irina

Enemies: Not disclosed

Suspicious activities as of now: Cousin – Shay

Reason for suspicion: Still unknown

It was around 8:00am, and the sun was still struggling to tear through the thick fog. Jai needed a smoke. He stepped out. Women draping themselves in shawls over sweaters were walking at a rapid pace from villas in the vicinity. Most of them had migrated to this city from West Bengal to work as part-time maids, while their husbands worked as carpenters, plumbers, etc. The city of Gurugram had employment for everyone. It accepted people from around the country. Jai called this group of people who were averting their gaze. They could spot a cop without a uniform and preferred to steer clear of them. Nervously, they came. Their network would put any detective agency to shame. They knew everything that was happening in the lives of the people who lived there.

They told Jai that the farmhouse was mainly vacant for the most part of the year, with the caretaker maintaining the house. But on the night of the 31st December, it seemed there was a small party. There was music, and the lights were on. While they did not see anybody, they assumed there must be some party as it was the last night of the year.

Jai felt satisfied about his initial work. It might not be a celebrity case, but it was high profile enough to land him a promotion. He smiled, imitating Agent Booth. The co-protagonist of the series that he watched some time back, "Bones[6]". Ever since, he had chanced upon "NYPD Blue[7]" as a teenager, he was addicted. The charisma of the detectives and cops caught his fancy and became his inspiration. Eventually, Jai had found his goal in life. Police procedural drama became his ritual. He would watch a police procedural drama till he slept.

Today, standing in AV's farmhouse, looking out at the hypnotic magical morning of Gurugram, he felt like a detective that he had so often seen in the series.

---

[6] *Bones - American crime crime police procedural comedy-drama television.*
[7] *NYPD Blue – American police procedural television series set in New York City.*

Passion Inherited

Jai was penning down his approach, the sequence of interviews, if autopsy ruled anything but natural causes. His fair share of exposure to crime in real and reel life had told him that it was a Murder. A Murder One, as it would have been termed in television series. But unlike the series, he would not solve it in 42 minutes. This case would take time. He would need to talk to everyone associated with AV alone and at separate times. His intuition told him something was wrong, a link that eluded him.

Deep down, his gut said, it was a murder. If so, then what was the motive, and who had it?. His chain of thought was interrupted by Mona Kuttan, his colleague.

"Jai, the autopsy report has just come in."

"Well! What is it?"

"Her heart stopped beating, and she died."

"You mean, a natural death?" asked Jai as he walked up to Mona to look at the autopsy report.

"Nopes, Mr. Dectective Jai. Not a natural cause". Mona teased him. Jai and Mona were batch mates in the police academy. Seldom were both assigned to a single case. This case piqued Mona's interest. Mona liked working on cases that followed money and money trail. Jai enjoyed solving murder, kidnapping, and drugs related cases.

"You are enjoying this, Ms. Kuttan?" smiled Jai as he snatched the file from her hand.

Mona continued, "Jai, it's simple case of natural death when a heart stops beating. Sometimes, the heart can stop beating like mine does when I look at you."

Mona constantly flirted with Jai. Jai was a tall man with an athletic build. Hours of watching TV did not manage to get an ounce of fat on this guy. He was a fitness freak who would run for 3-5 km every day. Jai smiled; he was no stranger to female attention. He was a heartthrob in the police academy and now in the police station.

"Ms. Kuttan, if I were to date you, I would have to kill your husband. I don't date married women. And... I can't risk getting involved in a crime against a cop's family. Nopes, cops, will become my personal enemy. No way. Just loads of risks, Ms. Kuttan, to date you. I would instead turn my attention to Ms. AV."

"Ah! The dead girl wins" Mona faked a sigh as she continued, "Yes, the heart had stopped beating. The question is, why did it? What caused it?"

Mona stopped for some time.

"Continue..."

"Methylenedioxymethamphetamine! She died due to OD - Overdose of the drugs."

"Request the family for her medical history. Does Ms. AV have a history of drug abuse? The OD was due to meth. If I am not mistaken, it goes by the street name – 'Ecstasy'."

"Ecstasy!" Mona added dramatically, "Death due to overdose of Ecstasy! Not injected; it was given to her in liquid form. Which made it far more lethal ...."

"Did I add that there was alcohol in her system? But of course, everybody knows she was a teetotaler."

"Any evidence of sexual assault or activity?"

"No"

"I don't know, Mona, but something is not adding up. An Aphrodisiac as a poison of choice is unorthodox. Could it be accidental OD? Or somebody is covering up for something."

"How are you approaching this case, Jai?"

"Inconclusive. I need to have my interviews with all the persons of interest."

Jai sat sipping a cup of tea that Chotu[8] had placed it on his table barely a minute ago. Every four hours, Chotu would come to the Police station to recharge the cops with a cup of freshly made hot ginger tea. Unlike other's tables, Jai's table was squeaky clean, with files carefully stacked on the holder. A photo frame with a smiling photo of his mom and an idol of Hanuman[9].

Postmortem Report No. 361CD54 || Ref. No. 7296C-1-1-2021

Body Identified by: Mrs. Bijlee (Aunt)

---

[8] *Chotu – A small boy who works in tea stalls, assigned with the work of serving tea. Commonly called Chotu.*
[9] *Hanuman – Deity in Hindu mythology. He is a monkey God and an integral part of Ramayana.*

Jai skipped a few pages that contained details of the chain of custody. He knew it was not broken. Instead, he proceeded to the main content.

SCHEDULE OF OBSERVATION

A – GENERAL

1. Name: Abhishikta Vats
2. D/O – Siddharth Vats
3. Height: 5 ft 4 inches Weight: 49.6 kg Physique: Athletic
4. Special Identification Features (in an Unknown Body) NA
5. Post-mortem Changes present (**Rigor mortis is setting in, post-mortem lividity and putrefactive signs; stained blood vessels, greenish discoloration, odor, softening of eye-balls, exudation from nose and mouth, ova or flies, moving maggots, blebs over the body, peeling off the cuticle, loosening of hair, thorax and abdomen burst, separation of sutures of the skull, eye changes, adipocere, mummification.**)
6. External Appearance: condition of limbs – No bruises, eyes - dilated pupils, ears – No alien substance, nostrils – clear, mouth – traces of drugs, anus – clear, vagina, and urethra - clear. A rape kit was administered, but it was negative. No physical sign of any sexual activities.
7. Injuries – No Injuries

Jai skipped pages. He was looking for a specific portion, Anatomic Summary.

AUTOPSY PROTOCOL

Name of deceased: Abhishikta Vats

Anatomic Summary:

I. Dilated and Hypertonic Cardiomyopathy

  A. Cardiomegaly (750 gm.)

  B. Left ventricular hypertrophy, heart (2.3 cm.)

  C. Congestive Hepatomegaly (2750 gm.)

  D. Congestive Splenomegaly (350 mg.)

II. Acute opiate Intoxication

  A. Acute passive Congestion – all Viscera

III. Toxicology (Separate Report)

Conclusion (Cause of Death) –

1. Dilated and Hypertrophic Cardiomyopathy
2. Acute Opiate intoxication

Jai circled the Acute Opiate intoxication in his copy. He pulled out his notebook that recorded his initial observation of the crime scene and browsed through the pictures in a loop, trying to connect the autopsy report with the physical crime scene.

Some questions were troubling him - Ecstasy is not an off the shelf available drug, nor were there no signs that AV took drugs, even for recreation. Was it an accidental OD for a first-timer? Or was it a deliberate suicide? Her people were behaving bizarrely. Was this behavior an indication that somebody was covering up a murder?

Mona entered with a young man with strongly built arms. She led him to Jai and moved to her table to leaf through a magazine. The young man was sunburnt with a sharp pair of eyes. He was the caretaker of the farmhouse, Neer. He stood standing, facing Jai with his palms folded.

"So, you are the caretaker. How old are you?" Questioned Jai.

"Around 37"

"How long have you been serving as caretaker?"

"Around 7 years"

"Now, listen to me keenly, and answer truly…." Jai fumbles to remember the name, and Neer fills in, "Neer."

"Yes Neer, where were you on the night of 31st Dec?"

"Saheb [10], I know nothing! Please spare me. I am innocent."

"Why do you think that there is crime here?"

"I know nothing, Saheb."

"Why do I find it difficult to believe you?"

"I am innocent and have nothing to do with madam's death. I was not there?"

"Do you have any idea, any notion at all, that to how easy it is to implicate you in this murder?"

Jai had no motive for implicating Neer. He was unsure if it was a murder, but Neer's nervousness exposed him as a weak link. Jai knew that Neer was hiding something.

---

[10] *Saheb – Sir.*

"I am a poor man, Saheb. Why do you want to trouble a poor man?" Neer wailed.

"Look here, Neer. I am in haste to find who is behind all this. I don't care if he is innocent or otherwise. All I want is that I take some name in the press conference and close this case."

Jai was acting the part of a 'bad cop' perfectly. He managed to get a crooked smile as he munched on a half-eaten apple. He was building pressure on this man who knew something but was unwilling to come forward. He was a frightened man looking for his survival and well-being. Accusing him of murder will make him spill everybody's secret. He needed that kind of leverage to get going with his theories.

"Well Neer, if not you, then who is it?"

"I have no idea Saheb. I was not there", Neer added hesitatingly, "That afternoon around 4 o'clock, Ma'am said she didn't need for my services for the day. I was free for the whole night. I was to report to duty the next morning at 6:00."

"But then you planned to come back sooner and kill AV."

Neer looked bewildered, "I reached the farmhouse around 5:00 in the morning. I had no idea that Ma'am was killed there. I thought she was enjoying the 31st Dec night. The music was on. I swear Saheb, I was not there when she was killed."

Twice Neer said she was killed. He was shocked when Jai named him as the accused, but AV being murdered did not come as a shock for him.

Jai leaned and whispered to Neer, "then, where were you?"

He stopped, and then nervously, he went on, "It was the 31st night, the last night of the year, so I decided to have some fun. I went to the city to enjoy myself. But I came back early. It was a bad night. I reached the farmhouse around 5 am."

"Bad night? What do you mean by it?"

"Well, er.. um... I mean.. a.. er.."

"What!" Jai asked sternly. Neer got startled and instantaneously added,

"Well Saheb, I lost money in drinking and gambling."

"Lost Money? What's your salary?"

"It was the whole saving of the year and some occasional tips."

Something in Neer's eyes said that he was lying. Jai did not pursue the matter anymore for the moment; it could wait. He could get any information from a coward like Neer whenever he wanted. Neer almost ran away from the Police Station after being dismissed.

"Mona Kuttan, what do you feel? Is the man to be trusted?"

"You let him go so easily Jai; Why? You had him squealing like a disgusting farm mouse. He would have shared everything he knew with a slightly more pressure."

"Yes, he knows something. But I intend to get to the real person behind this. Have I had pressurized Neer, it would have sent warning bells to the person involved, and he might try a cover-up?"

Pushing weights, Jai's mind was occupied with the most pertinent aspects of the case.

Would he treat it as a suicide or a murder? If he treats it as a suicide, then where is the suicide note? The choice of drug was unusual. Would it be easier to rule it as accidental OD? Then what if it was not? The victim had no history of drug abuse, then was there a foul play? And if it was a murder, then what is the motive? It would not be as easy a case as it appeared in the morning of 1st Jan. It needs thorough investigation. The question was, what line of questioning and interview to pursue?

AV had asked Neer to take the evening off. Why? Would a caretaker be a hindrance to a suicide plan? The maids said there seemed to be a party. Was she expecting someone? Who could that person be? Was he the person who got Ecstasy for her? Was Neer in reality absent from the property on that day? How would a caretaker have money to spend the night of the year drinking and gambling? He was given money by someone. Was he given hush money?

AV was taunting him with her death. She smiled sarcastically at the world that gave more importance to the dead than the breathing ones. In her end, she seemed to have won. She was compelling Jai to know her as a person when she was alive.

A section in the newspaper was devoted to AV. The brief news section indicated that the owner of the theme chain of hotels, Cena Cosmica, was found dead on the morning of 1st Jan. The body was discovered by her uncle and aunt. Police have not ruled it as a suicide. They are investigating and are expected to share the report soon.

A smile emerged on Vivaan's lips. It was shocking for him that he could be relieved reading about somebody's death. Guilt and happiness gripped his heart. He looked out of his Mercedes; the traffic was slightly thinner near Fortis Hospital. It was unusual. Neither was this day for him. Vivaan had to go straight to Huda Central City, but he changed his mind. He asked his driver to take him to Sheetla Mata Temple.

The driver was shocked. It was unusual for Vivaan Khatri to go to the temple on his way to the office.

"Sir, the traffic will be bad today for a ceremony in the temple. You will get delayed. I can take you in the evening."

"Don't worry about the time. Take me to the temple to visit Mata, to pray and thank her."

Vivaan sounded worried and relieved. He always had unwavering confidence, even in the face of loss that he was incurring due to the AV chain of a theme restaurant. At one point, Vivaan's 'Gourmet' was the most profitable restaurant chain. Then unexpectedly Cena Cosmica became a favorite haunt for lovers and corporate parties alike. Gourmet was incurring a loss. AV's passion was the secret sauce to Cena Cosmica's success. None of her competition could match the sheer intensity of AV's passion for her work. Vivaan stood smiling in front of the deity Sheetla. Life had given him another chance. It was unclear who would take care of Cena Cosmica; Dr. Divyansh was always in some scientific discovery of his. Bijlee was a good-for-nothing woman, and Shay was a spoilt brat. The person who had any sense of business that was AV. She inherited her resilience and business acumen from her father, Siddharth Vats. There was mutual rivalry and admiration between Vivaan and Siddharth. Once or twice a month in social gatherings, they would meet. That was how far their friendship went. Closing his eyes, he was ardently praying that fate would side with him this time.

Years ago, Siddharth was on the verge of bankruptcy. The market did not have much faith in Siddharth's concept of a theme restaurant based on astronomy. Still, Siddharth kept on pumping money into his passionate venture. Unluckily, nobody was willing to help Siddharth. Vivaan was waiting for Siddharth to fail. His plan was to acquire Cena Cosmica at a throw-away cost, but his dreams could not materialize. At the eleventh hour, Siddharth could pull some investments from his Australian connections that saved his venture.

AV was a girl of four at that time. She would always accompany her father on weekends to the restaurant and spend the whole day. Siddharth felt proud that Abby was inheriting his passion. His girl of four would play in the kitchen, boss the staff, and pick the special dessert of the day. Her father knew his dream Cena Cosmica was in safe hands, and his daughter displayed leadership qualities.

The Court Case

Siddharth managed to revive Cena Cosmica, and he put it on a fast track to success. He hired interior designers and special effects specialists. They converted a restaurant with a painted solar system on the ceiling to a magical step into the space effect. A step into the restaurant was like walking in space amidst stars. Vivaan, who had earlier laughed at this concept with his peers, had started to feel the brunt of Siddharth's success. From a minimum of 3 days, advance booking Gourmet's tables became available in walk-ins. Vivaan had started incurring a steady decline in profits as Cena Cosmica became the most talked about theme restaurant in NCR.

Time passed; life gave him another chance some years ago. 10 acres of land were sold by a realtor to both Vivaan and Sidharth. Both Vivaan and Siddharth wanted to build a theme resort. The agent disappeared with the sum of money, leaving both locked in a legal fight.

Vivaan and Siddharth went to court instead of an 'out of court settlement.' Siddharth was represented by Shabbir Amin, the town's best advocate, while the Vivaan was represented by Ihit Basu. Ihit was a sharp edge of a new knife. He had a deliberated approach coupled with a strange obsession to win in a courtroom. He seldom went for an out-of-court settlement. To win, he was ruthless in court, would play with the witness, and create parallel storylines with a single motive. If it needed a witness to be discredited, so be it. He never hesitated to destroy lives if they stood in his way.

Like any property case in NCR, the property case kept dragging. It was a case that became a synonym for the ego of Vivaan and Siddhart. Vivaan and Siddhart were fueling their lawyers to either win or ensure that the former party does not succeed. The game was of patience. None of the sides gave in, and the lawyers on each side ensured the previous side did not win. After 4 years, a ray of hope appeared for Vivaan. Siddharth had met with an accident. He had a daughter, turned 18, out of college, happy go lucky girl with no formal training or experience to run a chain of restaurants. Vivaan's proposal for an out-of-court settlement and friendly takeover of the restaurants was met with a deafening silence. Vivaan thought it was just a matter of time. He would have been contented to wait for Cena Cosmica to shut down or look for a takeover. Vivvaan's wait did not take long. Siddharth passed away almost after six months in ICU. And as per his will, Cena Cosmica fell in the hands of Abhishikta, or Abby, a girl just out of college with no experience in handling a business.

Vivaan's hope of buying out Cena Cosmica came crashing down. Soon he realized that he had underestimated Abby. She proved to be more challenging than her father. She was like a young general on a mission. She worked like she was living on borrowed time, slipping fast from her clutches, and she had to reach somewhere before her fist was empty. Vivaan had met Abby once or twice, and all of the times, she would nod and answer in a syllable or two.

Abby was a woman of action with a steely gaze that would penetrate the soul. Little did Vivaan know that behind that cold composure was a conspiring mind.

The court case took a strange turn after Siddharth's death. Abby's advocate went soft, and Ihit won the case with ease. He knew not that his victory was authored by Abby. Jubilant Vivaan was on his way to Ihit's office to celebrate. He was so impressed by Ihit's victory that he was ready to appoint him as his legal counsel for the next 3 years. Until that date, he was on a temporary contract which ended the moment Ihit won or lost the case.

For the past two years, Ihit had been following Vivaan to appoint him as the legal counselor of Gourmet. Ihit knew of the fine job he was doing, and he knew he deserved the position. But Vivaan had read his desire to win. Making him a legal advisor meant he would have to be on the payroll with the usual benefits. With the present arrangement, Ihit cost a fraction of what he would have. Ihit could not leave a case without winning. Ihit had won; it was time to retain him. To keep him by his side, he would have to offer what was due to him for a long time. Stuck in Iffco Chowk's traffic, Vivaan was humming the theme song of his favorite FM station, not realizing a man on a bike was following him. He knocked on the window as Vivaan gingerly rolled down the glass. He confirmed Vivaan's name and served with a notice. Cena Cosmica had appealed in a higher court against the decision. Vivaan rushed to Ihit's office, sipping his black tea by the window.

"Ihit! See what a fool this AV is? She went to the higher

court. This time Ihit, obliterate her. Destroy her so that she would not dare cross my path again."

"Well! Mr. Vivaan, it will be apt if you ask your advocate."

"I am asking my advocate."

"No, my contract with you is over."

"Okay, draft your contract, and I'll sign it. What's more, I am appointing you as my legal counselor."

"I am afraid it is too late and too little; if I may add. So I have accepted to work for someone else."

"You left me without informing me!"

"As per our agreement, after I won your case and collected my check from your accountant, our association is over. I am not contractually obliged to inform you who my next client will be. Still, for your satisfaction, I am a legal counselor to Ms. AV."

Vivaan could not comprehend what he was hearing. Ihit, who had won a case for him against AV, had joined her. It made no sense. He felt the bitter bile of betrayal and defeat in his mouth.

"Just tell me, how could you take up their case? They are our opponent!"

"Not anymore. I was on your side, represented the case justly, and once the case was resolved, the opposite party is no longer my opponent. I hold no personal grudge against them. The offer was good. I would have been a fool to let it go. But there is a difference. I am not representing Cena Cosmica. I am Ms. AV's legal advisor. That's it."

"So, it is solely about money. How much money do you want to join me?"

"Sorry, Mr. Vivaan, I have an agreement with Ms. AV to be with her for the next 5 years."

"Ihit, let me warn you, I will not let you represent them after you have worked with me. You were my advocate, privy to my business secrets. I will have court stop you. It will give them undue advantage over me."

"Relax, Mr. Vivaan. You are protected by advocate and client privilege. I cannot use any of the information I obtained while working with you in this or, in any case against you. If you do find something like that, you can have my license canceled. Again, you are protected by the law. Now, Mr. Vivaan, it is unwise for you or me to discuss matters that pertain to the case without your counsel present."

Vivaan left with yet another defeat. He hated losing, and as fate would have it, he kept failing to Cena Cosmica. First, it was to Siddharth and then to his young daughter AV. This was the beginning. In the next 2 years, Cena Cosmica won the property case. Within the next 2 years, the Cena Cosmica prospered under Abby. The person Vivaan dismissed as a 'mere kid' turned out to be his nightmare.

Abby pumped additional energy into her work sphere and brought several innovative ideas. She introduced Role Play on demand. Never hesitated to take a risk, she was amply rewarded. Soon, she left all the competitors behind to reach the top. This 'mere kid', Abby, had dethroned Vivaan. It was a wound that had not yet healed in years.

With Abby gone, he must get back to his top position. A knock made Vivaan look up from his laptop. Inspector Jai was at the door. When he read about Abby's death and foul play not being ruled out, he knew he would expect the police. Some tabloids were bringing in a conspiracy theory. Someone wanted to eliminate the entire family. The accident case of Abby's father, Siddharth, was still unresolved. Then, on the 1st Jan morning, Abby was also found dead under mysterious conditions. Vivaan was prepared for this sort of interview.

Jai came in and took a seat opposite Vivaan. Nothing escaped his keen eyes. Vivaan was perhaps in his late forties, but he had maintained well. Though his hair growth indicated a grey streak under a layer of dark tan. His height, lean structure with a sunken cheek - gave him a hungry look. The amber-grey eyes with two gold-plated left upper incisors and premolar gave him a vampirish look. And greed reflected in his pig-like narrow eyes. It was the eyes of a person who would never forgive his enemies.

"What can I do for you, officer?" Vivaan asked

"I came here seeking some information on Ms. AV."

"AV, I am afraid I was never friendly with her to give you any information. As you know, we had a healthy rivalry."

"That is why I came here" Jai paused, seeing Vivaan's face lose its color. Soon, he got himself back and, with ease, carried on.

"I don't understand exactly," emphasizing the 'exactly'.

"Distance sometimes gives us a improved sense of things. As rivals, I am persuaded to believe you must have had a watch on her."

"It's normal in our world. What's wrong with it?"

"Nothing. I just wanted to use some information you have acquired."

"At a personal level, I don't have any information."

"Sure, can you tell me what she was in her professional world? What was her working style?"

"Take by surprise. AV would take such risks as nobody else would dare. AV was such a gusty and feisty young girl. And her luck was always with her. She would make suicidal decisions, yet somehow she would come out of it with flying colors."

"What kind of person was she?"

"AV was someone who could peep into somebody's mind. She was elegant and charming. She had a knack for making people do anything she wanted." Then, quitely, he repeated as if he was confirming it to himself. "AV had a talent for making people do things she wanted them to do. And they would do it willingly and without any complaints."

"Any underworld connection?"

At this question, Vivaan was uncomfortable and uneasy.

"Well! Er...I mean, these things are done undercover … so …anyway, it's common and part of life now a day.

But, I mean, maybe or may not. I am not sure."
That was all Jai could get from Vivaan Sharma.

Motive & Intent

Dusk never creeps. Strands of yellow or orange would appear on a slender piece of sky peeping through the tall building. Then within minutes, darkness would descend. Shay waiting in his car, parked in a lane in the corner of Mahira's home. He was smoking one cigarette after another. When Mahira had called him, Shay sounded furious. She suggested he pick her up and spend the evening with her.

Mahira Sanya was Shay's yet another love at first sight. That was three years ago. Like star-crossed lovers, they were never destined to meet, but then they met. Ever since each moment, their feeling grew more and more intense. Somehow, almost every day, they managed to steal hours to spend together.

"I hope all the rituals for Abby are completed. May God give her soul peace.", Mahira said, adjusting her seat belt.

"I hope not," Shay replied, reversing his Ferrari.

"Shay! don't speak ill of the dead. They can't defend themselves. It's wrong."

"Mahira, Abby does not deserve any sympathy. At least your sympathy."

"She was your cousin. Your family."

"That is my misfortune. I would have been so nicer if I had not been a member of this dysfunctional family."

"All normal families are dysfunctional, varying by some degree or the other. Don't let anybody tell you otherwise."

Shay smiled sarcastically. Wondering to what extent he could share his family's dark and dirty secrets.

I wish I could tell you, Mahira, the dark secrets of my family.

"Somehow, I can't help feeling responsible for the rift between you and Abby," Mahira added as they drove.

"It's not you, Darling. Abby would have reacted alike to any girl in my life. That cold-hearted bitch could not get into any relationship and could not bear to see anybody being blissful in one."

Mahira had met Shay at Abby's party. Feeling out of place and visibly bored, Mahira was doodling on the tissue papers when Shay saw her. She looked refreshingly atypical in her white churidar [11] with bandhini[12] dupatta[13], sitting at a corner table as far as possible from the crowd sipping her mocktail and doodling something. Abby had invited her, but being a host, she could not make much time for Mahira. She introduced her to a couple of her friends, but Mahira had nothing in common with them. They spoke of the market, business, and profitability, and Mahira knew the language of colors. It was in one of the art exhibitions

---

[11] *Churidar - tight trousers worn by people from South Asia, typically with a kameez or kurta.*
[12] *Bandhini - Bandhani, (aka Bandhej); it is a type of tie and dye textile. Derived from the Sanskrit word 'Banda', - meaning 'to tie.*
[13] *Dupatta - a length of material worn arranged in two folds over the chest and thrown back around the shoulders, typically with a salwar kameez, by women from South Asia.*

when Abby met Mahira. One corner of the gallery was themed 'Hope and Love' by some debut painter. As expected, it was a neglected section. The colors caught Abby's eyes. When the coordinator called Mahira, informing 3 of her 7 paintings displayed in the gallery were sold, she almost choked on the tea. Throwing the cup, she almost ran from the street opposite the gallery. She ran in to see who the generous benefactor was. But by that time, Abby had left, leaving her contact details for her. Abby and Mahira could not meet for 2-3 months, and when they met, it was like two friends meeting. Since then, Mahira and Abby have been friends and manage to meet once a month or two.

With Abby's death, Mahira lost a patron and a friend. "I suppose Shay; Abby would have changed her mind about us. She just needed time to process."

"She would never have. She could afford being a warm and lovable patron of art. That would give her a beautiful cover story. That is what she was to you but remember how she behaved when she found out about us. That is what she was. The patron's image suited her, which is what you felt about her. But, sorry to say, the mask slipped in our final meeting. Don't you ever forget that."

"Yeah," Mahira continued sadly. Her lips twitched, and her big dark eyes trying best to hold a drop of tear that was forming there. She was blinking fast to disperse it. "She called me to the office. I was shocked to see such a another person."

"That was real, Abby. I hate her. And I am glad she is dead. When I told Abby about our relationship. All hell broke loose. She accused me of being a good-for-nothing chap who goes on wasting hard-earned money."

Abby's words were ringing in Shay's mind.

Since how long Shay, have you been going around with Mahira. You want to marry off this girl but tell me what you are if you subtract your title of Vats from your name. You are known because you are AV's cousin. Without me, you are just a graduate who has not shown any interest in further studies or in joining the family business.

Shay was silent. He had a ambient noise in his head. Abby's voice, the voices of friends, and the voices of the past.

You are just interested in wasting money that you have not earned. First, start making money instead of fooling around with girls on the money earned by others. You are wealthy today. Who can assure you that you will always remain so? You are an irresponsible person who is a burden to himself and now wants to add another. Before you add another person to the family, create your credibility and your financial status.

Mahira squeezed Shay's hands. She could sense Shay's pain.

"Her words, those icy spine-chilling words, are still haunting me. I just hate her, Mahira. That day, she called you into her office. She did every possible thing to break our relationship."

"I was appalled to find a new Abby. She started firing her questions, ... you know Shay, her exact words were,"

"Why are you attracted to Shay, Mahira? Neither is he handsome nor is he earning. A wasteful creature he is, always zooming in and out in flashy cars. You are a sensitive person. You are an artist; how could you get attracted to a pompous and vain person like Shay. Is it truly love or a shortcut to the limelight? Tomorrow, if Shay begs on the streets, will you still love him? If yes, here is a pre-nuptial agreement declaring that you would have no claims on his money. Your personal expenses will be out of your own earnings, not earnings of Shay's or his inheritance. ......"

Shocked, Mahira threw the paper, "I have been humiliated enough. Neither will I sign this nor leave Shay. Do what you got to do".

"So, you are after money, Mahira?" Abby asked in disbelief.

"Take it anyways you like."

"Remember, between you and Shay's money, which is technically my hard-earned money, it is me, AV. I hope you remember what I am called in the circle, a Bitch who wins. Don't you forget this!"

That was the ultimate meeting between Mahira and Abby. For the next few months, Mahira tried her best to reason with her changed attitude but could come up with no theory. Maybe, Abby was whatever one thought her to be.

Shay and Mahira were walking hand in hand under the green canopy of Leisure Valley. The silence was soothing. It was comforting after the stir Abby's death created.

After a long silence, Mahira asked, "Why do you think Abby was so much against love?"

"Who can say? Maybe she was plain jealous because she had never found love. That's why she could not stand seeing someone else in love."

Shay was as bitter as he was on the day of Abby's death. Death tends to revive glorious memories and obliviate the painful ones. Not for Shay. He could not forgive Abby even after her death. Anger was consuming Shay like venom. At every opportunity he found, Shay lashed out at Abby. Mahira had never seen such darkness in Shay. It frightened her momentarily. Shay continued, "Only an insane man can love such a proud and haughty girl. She never knew what love was. All Abby cared for was a success. Drunk with success, she believed she was the God of our fates. Being loveless and successful does that. I, for one, am glad that she is dead."

"I feel a bit sad for her."

"Aha! Forget her. Abby does not deserve any sympathy."

"Everybody does. There is enough hurting. You have to let Abby go in peace."

"I hope she never gets peace. It is appropriate that she died; else, I would have killed her. Remember, she was the one who stood between us. Now that she is no more, I am free. We both can marry off. Father won't stand in our path now. Whatever happened, happened for good."

"Don't implicate yourself by uttering such a foolish thing. Abby was your cousin, and now she is dead under mysterious circumstances. Police have not yet ruled it as a suicide. Don't attract unnecessary attention to yourself."

Shay's grip tightened. It began hurting Mahira's hand. He turned towards her and said, "Look here love, it's you and me together, now and forever. Anyone standing between us is dead. If a blood bath is needed to win, I will not hesitate."

Mahira, could not say anything, she opened her mouth to perhaps say something, but words failed. A stranger was wearing Shay's face. He seemed ruthless. Standing on the fringe of insanity and darkness, the man seemed to enjoy the call of the Abyss and falling through it.

"You have no idea Mahira, how much I love you and to what extent I can go for our love."

The night was smoggy. The smoke of burning dried leaves added to the smog. Air was both moist and singed. Too much was going on in their minds. Moments of peace and green would help. They sat on the grass for a long time, feeling the love and trying to forget Abby.

Shay and Mahira stopped at a restaurant for dinner on their way back. Smiling and laughing, they entered. Unknown to them, inspector Jai also happened to be there. He was with his friends. After Shay and Mahira were seated comfortably and placed the orders, Jai went to them and introduced himself.

"Mr. Shay Vats, I am inspector Jai. I hope you remember. We met on the 1st of Jan. You were too high to remember. May I join you and this lovely lady?"

"Please do so."

"Actually, I wanted to ask you about your cousin, but you were not sober enough to speak. However, I see you have recovered from the shock of your cousin's death."

"Ah…well …. Er…er…. Birth and death are part of life. One must take it normally."

"Yes, and you have taken it well. Just two days have passed since AV's death, and you are here in a restaurant having a fancy dinner."

"Last time I checked, it is not a crime," Shay added with irritation.

"Everybody grieves differently, officer," Mahira said, trying to diffuse the building tension; she was worried that Jai would sense the darkness in Shay that she had seen today.

"We have discovered some fingerprints and …" Jai took a well-calculated pause to gauge Shay's face lose its color and compose. Then he continued, "and we would appreciate any help from you. It would expedite the case if you could help us with a sample print tomorrow for our reference for elimination."

Shay nodded. Jai left for this group with a smile of satisfaction. Shay's activities were disturbing and were highly suspicious. Jai was triumphant to ruin Shay's evening mood and plans, whatever they may have been.

Dr. Divyansh Vats was looking at something under the microscope when inspector Jai knocked. Annoyed, Dr.

Divyansh replied without looking up. "I said, I don't want to be disturbed. Go, I don't want any tea."

"Dr. Divyansh ..." in a slightly lower voice, Jai called. The surprised doctor looked up to find Jai at the door. Jai continued, "Sorry to disturb you. I could not resist the temptation to come here when I was told you were here. After all, it is not often one can see a famous scientist at work. Can I see any bacteria or virus mounted on the slide?"

Dr. Divyansh was upset to find inspector Jai but decided not to express it. "As you see, I am in the middle of an experiment, Officer. It could be dangerous. I am nearing completion, which means I am swamped and will not be free for the next hour. If you can wait for about an hour, I will finish the experiment and then can show you some slides. Now, if you will excuse me."

Saying this, he turned towards the corner table and suddenly, as if he remembered something, "Please do not do your own experiment here. Some chemicals here can take your life."

"Don't worry, I won't mess with anything. I would just look around."

The first floor of the left wing was converted into a lab. There were 14 tables on both sides and a door linking to another room where animals were kept. A thought crossed Jai's mind if it was legal to use animals there for any experiments. The doctor was deeply involved in his work. He had prepared some solutions. He took some in a syringe and went to the room where animals were kept. Jai looked around the tables and racks, reading the labels on the neatly arranged containers. He kept reading 'Acetic Acid, Anhydrous sodium bicarbonate' and some more tongue twisters labels. Then he started the list with alphabet B, 'Barium, Bismuth, Boric Acid' smiling to himself, he moved from one table to another.

'Lead,....methyl hydroxide, methylenedioxymethamphetamine', molybdenum .... Wait .... what ... methylene-di-oxy-methamphetamine! Liquid Ecstasy'

It was a clean and transparent liquid.

He nearly dropped the bottle when he heard the doctor's voice.

"Well, Inspector! I hope you have not invented something now."

The doctor seemed to be in an excellent mood.

"Not exactly. I was going through the tongue twister names."

Dr. Divyansh took Jai to another room, where he showed him some slides of viruses and bacteria. Again, Jai displayed a genuine interest in science which somehow pleased Dr. Divyansh. Next, they went into the living room with Dr. Divyansh, explaining why the virus was considered an organism at the edge of life, a border between the world of living and nonliving.

In the comfort of the living room, Jai began speaking.

"Doctor, could your sister join in. I have some important information to share."

"Bijlee has gone out. She would join us in half an hour. I would update her. Officer, please continue."

"The cause of Ms. AV's death, according to the autopsy report, is an overdosage of

methylenedioxymethamphetamine."

Jai paused to judge the confused look on the doctor's face. The doctor was silent, and there was precipitation on his forehead.

"Would you have any idea as to how this chemical found itself in her drink?" Jai continued

"I have no idea."

"I would ask you to think before you answer. Did Ms. AV have a history of drug abuse, or was she friends with somebody who used?"

"I am not certain if Abby had friends. She was obsessed with her work, and that was her world. I can't say I know any of her friends who used drugs."

"Did you ever suspect her of using drugs or being depressed or suicidal?"

Dr. Divyansh shifted uncomfortably in his chair. He avoided looking at Jai.

Abby was in trouble when she was alive and when is dead.

"Officer, no idea about Abby's friends or if she was suicidal. She was mercurial and moody. I cannot say what was in her mind."

"Is this chemical freely available?"

"Not that freely."

"Did she have a history of drug use, or was she a recreational user?"

Again, the same question is put differently. This rookie cop thinks repeating the question in a different way will get different answers. How naïve!

"She was not an addict. No!"

Dr. Divyansh was knitting his brows. Trying to think hard.

Are they suspecting that Abby was murdered?

"Do you think, Officer, someone spiked her drink?"

"At this point, I can't rule out anything."

"I don't think someone was there in the farmhouse." Dr. Divyansh tried to confirm.

"As I said, I am ruling out nothing. I am checking all possibilities. Did Ms. AV leave a will?"

"Not sure. Abby never discussed this with us. If she left a will, it should be with her advocate, Ihit Basu."

The family was not close.

"In absence of her will, to whom does the property go?"

"According to my brother's will, after him, the property went to his daughter, Abby. Bijlee and I would have our boarding and lodging expenses taken care of. Plus, a modest allowance for our personal expenses. Yes, Abby included Shay in the allowance. In her father's will, it is stated that if Abby died without a will, the properties and all her assets would be handed over to a trust."

"And who are the trustees?"

The doctor was uncomfortable again, "Both Bijlee and

I."

There comes a twist.

"In short, you and Ms. Bijlee have full control over Ms. AV's properties. A nice change from what you said, a modest allowance to being co-owner."

Before Dr. Divyansh could reply, to his relief, Bijlee came in. Jai asked her

"Ms. AV was going somewhere. Where and Why? Do you have any idea?"

"Abby told me that her life was going to change. But no one knew her plans. She lived a strange life; she had no one intimate with her. Never shared what was in her mind or heart."

"Well, you know Aunt Bijlee. I can call you Aunt, right. You remind me of a distant aunt of mine… Coming back to the topic, Aunt Bijlee, is this not strange that none of you ever had a clue what was happening in Ms. AV's life. You, who are her family and stand to gain by her death, have no clue about her personal life! I am a officially intrigued." Jai added, ambling across the room.

"She was a Sphinx since her father's death. Her actions were not easy to comprehend. She was never like this. She was a loving, open, honest, carefree, jovial person whose sole motive was to be happy. After Sid's death, I mean, after Siddharth's death, she changed. She never smiled in the same way again."

"I need fingerprints from all family members for reference and elimination."

"Sure, you can have our fingerprints, but Shay is not

here. When he returns, I will have him meet you in your office", Dr. Divyansh replied.

Jai did not disclose that he had already met Shay in a restaurant and had asked him to drop by the police station for the fingerprints. In the equivalent way, he had simply forgotten to mention that a set of fingerprints was found on the doorknob and brass vase from the crime scene.

After Jai left, both Bijlee and Dr. Divyansh sat down, looking worried.

In his jeep, Jai was trying to figure out all possible solutions.

Shay's activities were suspicious. What could have been his motive? Further, Dr. Divyansh's motive could be money. His lab was full of sophisticated apparatus, not to mention they were costlier than his allowance. Was he funding his research from Ms. AV's pocket?

Jai's initial background search indicated that the doctor was a freelance, famous for his work but was not attached to any university. As a result, he could not get along with his colleagues or the universities.

Were his experiments proving costlier than his allowance, and that's why he needed control of AV's money. This is evident, what is hidden. Jai, think, think hard about what is not visible… What if AV fell in love and married somebody? Would that change the financial gain that the uncle and aunt were set to gain on her death?

Dr. Divyansh was a dedicated scientist who gave up his family life for his passion. His divorce was the talk of the town. He seemed overtly gratified of his decision to leave his wife, who demanded more family time, for his love of science. He became a target for feminist movements in the city for some days, and then people forgot about it. He had access to the liquid ecstasy.

Could it be that AV had decided something that would have hurt Dr. Divyansh's interest? Or could it be that somebody wanted to frame Dr. Divyansh? Somebody who was shrewd enough to know that the chemical was available in the doctor's lab.

A Lead

Back in the police station, inspector Jai was summoned by District Superintendent Narender Agarwal. He wanted an update on the case. Some of the posts on social media were getting viral. An unknown citizen journalist was floating the idea of a conspiracy.

Bade Saheb[14]! Jai thought. *Wants me to finish the investigation as soon as possible. Does not matter to him if all the ends are not neatly tied. As long as it does not implicate someone who can fight the system.*

The so-called discussion would go on. After about five minutes, Narender's eyes would continuously wander to the stock market. However, his face would not give a clue of his faking attention and interest in the case. He traded on his wife's behalf. All the transactions were in his wife's name. The issues brought to his notice were not as interesting as the money stock market would get him. And then would repeat things that Jai would have suggested as his brainchild and dismiss him.

Today it was different. Narender was being interviewed by a journalist for his initiatives against crime. Narender had managed to always twist the story in his favour. His promotions came more frequently as he traded one success story for another. He had a small team of

---

[14] *Bade Saheb – Big Boss. Generally, a boss with an inflated ego flaunting authority. Used as sarcasm and a nickname behind the person's back.*

friends and family who helped him create the best of the stories as an advertisement. And it has been successful to date.

Some media circus. Jai thought. He despised this man. He was everything an Officer should not be. Nevertheless, he smiled and nodded at the guest in the room. He promised exclusive of Ms AV's investigation, the expert salesman he was. The lady in front wanted her pound of flesh, an exclusive piece comprising all the details so subtly skipped from the news.

She smiled and stretched out her hand. "Hello, I am Asreet Kaur. I have been promised an exclusive by DSP, Narender."

Narender nodded, clearing Jai to share the investigations so far. Jai had learnt to put on a poker face. He was uncomfortable, but he hid it well from Asreet and his boss know.

Asreet continued, "Is it true that Ms AV was murdered?"

"At this moment, it is still inconclusive."

"Do you have a list of suspects?"

"Under the current circumstances, we cannot disclose any names. I hope you understand; it would affect the current investigations."

"How long will it take for police to decide between a murder or suicide? By the present speed, how many years will it take for police to book the suspect?", Asreet was provoking him to disclose anything.

"Ma'am, we are cops, not some freaking Superheroes.

We have our procedure. We would love to put culprits behind bars, but we do not have a mystical crystal ball to lead us straight to the murderer. Nor can we speculate like the media does."

Carry on Inspector Jai; at least you have confirmed that you are looking at the murder angle.

Asreet always had a way with words. Just the right amount of sarcasm and tone managed to have the right intended effect.

"We have to find strong evidence to arrest somebody. I am Jai Prakash Chautala, I don't let criminals walk under my watch, but then I don't even implicate innocent like you do. Now, as you say, we are lagging behind and need greater speed, so excuse me, I have to return to my investigations and files."

Narender nodded as Jai asked to be dismissed. True, he could not give the promised exclusive to Asreet, but the modest show that Jai put up was worth cashing in someday.

Crime scene photographs were spread on his table. Jai looked at them and then closed his eyes to remember the house as it felt and examined when he went there. Everything was in order, perfect. A side table near her bed had a glass containing apple juice. The juice was spiked with Liquid Ecstasy. Some bowls and one of the plates were greased in the kitchen. House indicated absence of any struggle. All doors and windows were open.

What was odd in this perfect scene? Was it an accidental OD case? In that case, why would AV not call somebody for help? Her phone records did not show any call near the time of her death. Was it a murder? What was missing? A struggle!

Jai was creating the scene in his mind.

The killer was known to her. Someone she trusted. The perp knocked on the door. She opened the door, and, seeking the opportunity, the killer spiked her juice smoothly. The meth did its work. She had a flight at dawn. Before the meth could start showing symptoms, she would have sunk in her bed to have winks of sleep.

While waiting for the fingerprints to match, he planned to interrogate Neer and interview Irina. Jai was convinced that this coward knew something, and he would sing like a canary with the proper pressure tactics.

Irina was arranging files in AV's office when inspector Jai came in. She had a dark, smooth, and attractive skin tone, giving her eyes more light. She had a pleasing personality. She was visibly disturbed.

"You look too disturbed. Is it for Ms AV's death?"

"Yes"

"How long have you been her personal secretary?"

"Three months after she took over the business, I joined her"

"Now what? Is your job affected by AV's death?"

"I have no idea. I may or may not have a job. Anyway, I would wait till the time the family comes up with any decision about the business. That would include my job as well."

"I do hope whatever is decided is best for you."

"Thank you, Officer. What brings you here?"

"I need some information. I am definite you can help me. But, first, how was Ms. AV as a person and boss?"

"In the business world, she was called 'a Bitch who wins'. I am uncertain if she knew what people called her behind her back. The truth is, she loved to win and had a knack for winning. When she took over the business, a crazy passion took over her. She wanted to expand her business. She fiercely protected and cared for her restaurants. Nobody dared to cross her path."

"How could she manage to take her restaurants to the top from the brink of disaster? Did she have any underworld contact? What was her secret recipe of success – any Godfather?"

"If she had a godfather, it was her determination and disciplined life. She could forgive errors in dictation but not in professionalism. She was too punctual. She personally came to the office at 8:55 am sharp and left after 7:00pm. In her introduction speech, I am told she said that she believed in hard work and punctuality and expected the consistent effort from everybody. She wanted everybody to be in by 9:00am. Some people took it as a mere introduction speech. After a few days, those who fell back to their routine of being late were fired. She was like an army General. She achieved a lot due to these qualities."

Jai leaned forward towards Irina. His voice was barely above a whisper.

"Look, Ms. Irina, what I am going to ask is a bit sensitive. You have to be meticulous. Tell me in detail. Do not leave any slight bit out. It may help us."

Irina nodded in agreement. Talking about Abby had calmed her a bit.

"What do you know about her personal life?"

"Her personal life – like?"

"Her relationship with others, relationship with her family?"

"Ask them. How do you expect me to know the internal family matters?"

Irina, slightly more, open up a bit more.

"Because, as far as I have learnt that you were more than her personal secretary. You were like her friend. Listen, would you not like to help us to solve this case?"

"Officer, I can land in serious trouble if any family member comes to know …."

"I can assure you that whatever we discuss here will not be shared. Your information will be used to search for evidence. The charge sheet will be filed based on the evidence and not the information shared by you. And your name will never be mentioned."

"Abby never spoke openly against any of them, but her relationship with them was under considerable strain. Then, one afternoon, I remember preparing coffee for Abby when Dr. Divyansh entered. He was burning with fury. I overheard the conversation. I can't remember the exact words, but the conversation went something like this …."

"You can't do this to me."

"I have not done anything that should not have been done."

"You have restricted the cash flow."

"I gave you a considerable amount of time to complete your project."

"Nobody in this world can predict when the experiment will be successful. That is why they are called experiments and not some damn boardroom meeting. Research takes time, but I am near completion. The patent will bring in huge money. Obviously, you will get a big share in it. You can build your business empire ten times over. Think about it, Abby. You can't give up now when we are in the endgame on verge of a major discovery."

"You had been an inch from the finale since… I don't know when … eternity. I can't keep funding you like this."

"It is not fair."

"It is not unfair. You will get the amount allocated to you by my father. As per inflation, the amount would be raised, but expect nothing more."

"Damn it! You don't understand. It's not enough."

"Can't help you."

"Abby, I need money. Give it to me as a loan."

"Uncle, I have the responsibility of running Cena Cosmica. I have to plan its expansion too. Please learn to live with what has been allocated for you."

"What is this penny for beggars? You know full well that I need some thrice of the amount allocated. What will your meagre amount do? All scientific discoveries need sacrifices."

"Uncle, sacrifice what is yours to sacrifice. You can't ask me to sacrifice for your cause and passion."

"I don't need your pity or charity. I need my part of the property."

"Uncle, you know for certain that you have no claim over Cena Cosmica. Father invested his saving from his salary to build this. He has not taken his share of ancestral property. He had transferred every bit of the property he had inherited to you and Aunt Bijlee. Yet, you want a portion of the property. Yes, legally, you have no share in his group. I am afraid there is nothing more I can do for you."

"You will regret this day, Abby."

"That was the conversation between Dr. Divyansh and Abby. Abby was distraught after this. After that day, she would avoid going home at 7:00pm. Even when the work was done for the day, Abby would stay back under some pretext. She avoided going home till late at night. After that, she got herself immersed in work. Sometimes, she would work for 24 hours straight."

"Those days did you accompany her for 24 hours, or you left after your shift"

"I had become attached to Abby. I used to inform my family and stay back to give her company. Her eyes would be red, but she would continue. Her pain gave her more energy. Still, warmly she would look up and tell me to leave and take a rest. She would insist that her driver would drop me home. When I refused, she insisted I catch winks of sleep and would wake me up when required. I used to sleep here in that siesta."

"When did this incident with Dr. Divyansh happen?"

"Some 4 months back."

"Did Dr. Divyansh ever come to this office after the incident?"

"4 Days before this tragedy...."

"Did you happen to know why? By chance, happen to hear something?"

"Yeah, I did."

"For money?"

"No, this time, it was for love."

"Love?"

"Shay and Mahira were having an affair and wanted to get married. Abby was totally against it. Shay was without a job, and Abby did help him with money from time to time over the allowance she allotted him. But Shay is not a trustworthy person. Abby never interfered with Shay's previous relationships, but in this case with Mahira, she put her foot down. Dr. Divyansh came here to convince her to accept their relationship."

"Did she accept it?"

"No!"

"Abby unambiguously stated that if Shay took a single step against her wish, she would sever all relationships with Shay and Dr. Divyansh. Dr. Divyansh stayed neutral, not wanting to take sides with his good-for-nothing son against his successful niece. He had no option, considering two additional burdens when he was already running short of cash for his experiments."

"So, they made peace."

"Likely."

"How was Abby's relationship with Shay and her aunt?"

"Regarding Aunt, I have not heard anything bitter or bad from Abby, but she was not chummy with her aunt. She was suspicious of her, I guess. She seldom spoke about people she disliked. Maybe Abby did not like Bijlee aunt that much."

"And Shay?" Jai asked.

"I have not seen Shay and Abby talking except on 31st Dec. Abby had canceled all her appointments and left for her farmhouse at 2:00pm. Shay came in around 3:15pm. He was arrogant, rude, and not to mention outraged. He asked me where she was, and when I told him, he left."

"Shay knew where Abby was that fateful day," Jai confirmed.

"Yes"

"When did you last see Abby?"

"That day, when she left for her farmhouse...."

An Arrest

The meeting with Irina was beneficial. Jai gathered plenty of details about Abby's life. Three days ago, she was just a name on his file, a case he needed to solve. Now, she appeared more human. For the preceding 4 months or so, Abby was distraught. Something was troubling her, but she kept it to herself. Her mood had changed entirely fifteen to eighteen days before her death. She appeared to be happy. She was excited, as if something was about to change her life. However, under the smile, there was something that pained her heart. She never disclosed it to anyone. Abby had planned to do something that was perhaps suitable for everybody. For that, she was going to Australia. Apart from this information, Irina could not give him any more details. She could not answer if the trip to Australia was for business or pleasure. Abby did not ask Irina to make the hotel bookings for the first time.

The Australia link turned out to be a dead end; instead Shay's angle had some juice, and so did Dr. Divyansh's.

Was it the son or the father? Both had motives. People had killed for a lot less! Were the father-son in on this together?

These two angles needed more investigation.

Out of curiosity, Jai once again affirmed if Abby had a secret love life. Irina confirmed that Abby did not have any love affair. She always took care of Abby's personal and official emails and appointments. She had never come across anything that would remotely suggest any love affair. However, the lack of love in her personal life was not the cause of her opposition to Mahira's and Shay's romance. As per Irina, Shay was a useless person who wanted to marry Mahira but did not want to take any responsibility. As per the picture painted by Irina, Abby was not a jealous person.

Was the image that Irina painted of Abby actual? The question kept biting Jai.

Jai was now convinced that the death of Abby was a murder. His years of experience was guiding him to choose murder over suicide. There were enough motives for murder. On the one hand, Dr. Divyansh needed money badly for his experiments. He knew about his brother's will. One would have assumed that Abby was too young to work on her will. It was Abby who stood as an obstacle between his passions, science. Abby's death would open the doors of wealth and control of Cena Cosmica. He would be the trustee and have an open hand in using funds. He could always manage to convince Bijlee for whatever he wanted as long as he gave her something she wanted in return. They were like two parasites in a symbiotic relationship. Abby was the one who was ruining his plans. He had also seen a vial of the chemical responsible for her death in Dr. Divyansh's lab.

Was Dr. Divyansh acting alone, or was there any accomplice with him? Was Shay working with him? Was it a common goal for which both father and son worked together? Both of them stood to gain from her death. Father would gain access to the money, and the son would get his love. It was time to get more dirt on the father-son.

It was time to interrogate Neer.

Neer was already nervous in a crampy interrogation room when Jai came in.

"So Neer, are you married?"

"Yes, my wife and one-year-old kid are in the village."

"I feel sorry for them."

"Why? Why do you say so? I have done no wrong."

"You are hiding someone adeptly. I know it was a murder, so that leaves you, Neer as my prime suspect. I present you to the world as the killer of Ms. Abhishikta Vats. Eventually, the media will be silent, and people will forget you soon enough. I can prove that you had enough motives for this crime and get a circumstantial conviction. I don't think you can afford a decent advocate. By the time you would come out of prison, your son would have a kid of 5 years. How does this sound to you?"

"Have mercy! Please don't frame me. You know Sahib, I am innocent."

"You would not look innocent to the judge. If I prove that you were on the property on 31st Dec, She was leaving for Australia, and you thought she would have loads of ornaments and cash. You crept in and were trying to steal. AV walked into the robbery, and you killed her."

Neer was sweating. His breath was rapid.

"Have you heard of third-degree?" Jai continued. He was trying to scare Neer. Dim-witted, Neer did'nt even try to figure out the extent of truth and scare tactics that Jai was using. He believed every word that Jai was telling him. And Jai was compelling in his act. "Third degree often makes an innocent confess to the crimes they have not committed. I can use it on you. So, let me ask you one final time, will you tell the truth or go to prison for life?"

"I will tell you the truth, nothing but the truth. Please believe me. I was swayed by my greed. I am a greedy pig, but I am not a killer."

"Okay, Neer, you are on records now. Give your statement."

Jai did not expect the turn of events. Neer was singing.

"Around 4:00 to 4:30pm, Shay Sahib went to the farmhouse. He kept on banging on the door until Ma'am opened it. She had dismissed staff for the day. Shay Sahib was furious; he was yelling. I was in my room, but I could hear everything. Hearing such a din and bustle, I went towards the door. The moment Ma'am opened the door, he almost strangled her. Before I could reach, Ma'am had freed herself. I peeped through the open window. She sat on the sofa while Shay Sahib kept pacing up and down.

The argument was about Shay Sahib's love life. He was trying his best to convince Ma'am that he loved Mahira. Nothing in the world would change his feeling for her. However, Ma'am was unmoved; she stood as a rock. She was not swayed at all by his pleadings. Shay

Sahib has a dirty past.

Ma'am was equally furious. She blamed him that he never had attached any emotional value to any of his past girlfriends. I often opened the farmhouse for Shay Sahib and his girlfriends. Shay Sahib was basically looking for an enjoyable time without any commitment. But that afternoon, he kept saying that Mahira had wholly changed him. He is not his usual self. It seemed that Ma'am did not trust anyone in the family. Ma'am told Shay Sahib that she had private investigators tailing all family members. I was shocked to hear this. How could Ma'am do this? Shay Sahib was enraged to find it."

Jai let Neer go. He wanted to go through the interrogations with Neer again. He closed his eyes to visualize the events between Shay and Abby that fateful afternoon.

"Abby, please consider your decision. Can't you see nobody is okay with this decision!"

"I don't sell candies. I can't keep everybody happy. But I know what is to be done. I have made up my mind."

"You can. Nobody dares stand against you because they fear you, not because they love you. We all live under the shadow of fear. We are afraid that something will change your mood, and we will be penniless."

"Then do as I say, cousin Shay."

"Shit! Damn it! Abby, Damn you! How can you be so cold? Do you have rock or ice instead of the heart? I stand corrected. I should rather ask, do you have a heart?"

"Shay, I can't have another girl's life ruined due to you. How conveniently have you forgotten that a girl went into trauma just because of you? She was a train wreck. She had a nervous breakdown; she was thrown out of her hostel. None of the colleges would give her admission. Such was the stigma. She could not face any interview for any job. You ruined her life, Shay. I will not let you do it all over again."

"I can explain it, Abby. We had an unquestionably 'no commitment relationship.' We were free to walk away without consequences or guilt whenever we liked. We both agreed, but then she wanted more from the relationship. I don't like to be chained. Despite all my warnings, she tried to chain me. I had to break it."

"So, break it again. It should not be difficult for you. Now that you have experience."

"What is it? Some kind of twisted revenge. I told you with Mahira, it is different."

"No! what ever happened to Hinal; I don't want to be repeated with Mahira. I don't want any more guilt in my heart. If you love her so much, break all your relationship with me and marry her. Take care of your responsibilities. Can you do that? No, as much as I know you, all you want to do is flirt and spend the money I earn."

"What is this bull shit? You just make everything about you. Stop all this nonsense about guilt and responsibility?"

"Have you forgotten Shay? Hinal was my friend. You met her through me. I did not intervene then as I thought you both were mature adults who could take care of yourselves. I had no idea that Hinal had such a tender heart. Once you broke her heart, it totally broke her. Again, you are repeating the history with Mahira. You met her at my party and shamelessly started flirting with her. Why you have to hunt for your next prey from my guest list? It is cheap. I would not let you destroy her life too."

"I am not the psycho that you are making me. You know for sure, Abby, this time it is different."

"Oh really! How is Mahira dissimilar from Hinal? To what extent can you go for Mahira? Can you leave everything for her? Your father can fall for this act, but not me. I know Shay, you will not change ever in your life, not for Hinal and not for Mahira."

"You have got father turned against son. My father would not dare annoy you with his precious project. You should remember this, dear cousin; blood is thicker than water. Do not try to break us apart. Benignly step aside from the matter that is not yours to be involved in, or else you will be responsible for anything that happens to you."

Jai intently watched the recording to find any signs that Neer had lied. Neer's narration went on, "Shay Sahib turned to leave. Some insanity got a hold of him near the door, and he took the heavy brass vase and hurled it at Ma'am. Luckily it missed her by some inches. He left murmuring, 'I will kill anybody who stands between Mahira and me'.

That afternoon, I was not supposed to be at home. I

had left before Ma'am came, but I had lost money and wanted to recover it. I sneaked back in. I saw Shay coming in when I was about to leave. I stuck around for a few minutes. I left around 5:00 pm. As luck would have it, I had lost all the money in gambling. I came back around 5:00 am. Ma'am was already dead by that time. Dr. Divyansh found some time in the din and bustle and asked me if Shay was there. I told him the truth. He was too anxious, asked me to keep my mouth shut, and he would double my salary and care for my son's education. A fool that I am, I thought that Dr. Divyansh would have become the next owner of Cena Cosmica. I did not find it wise to displease him. Saheb, please don't involve me in the murder, I am greedy swine, but I did not kill Ma'am."

Neer lied from the beginning. He went out at 4:00pm instead of 5:00pm.

Jai's plan worked. He got a star eyewitness in Neer. But, to make his case rock solid, he needed one more thing, forensic evidence, before he could arrest Shay. That evening fingerprint reports came in one set of fresh fingerprints matched with Shay. Within an hour or so, an arrest warrant was issued. Jai went towards Vat's House to arrest Shay.

The Challenge

As soon as inspector Jai arrested Shay, desperate calls were made to Ihit. Dr. Divyansh and Bijlee both kept on trying Ihit's number. His mobile was switched off. Every time, they received a similar reply. "Hi, please leave your message along with your name. Do not forget the number after the beep. Beep!". They tried the landline. It went to the answering machine. It was worse than they could have imagined. Each minute weighed down like mountains. They felt so helpless and looked as if fate had conspired against them.

Again and again, they left messages on the answering machine.

The quiet house was dark. Waiting for people to return.

Around 12:10 am, Ihit's car entered. Out stepped a tall man in a black suit from a long line of advocates. Practicing law was his family business. Although most of them settled around Kolkata or Calcutta, Ihit chose to move to Gurugram, much to the dismay of his family. He parked his car in his garage and opened the door to his bungalow in sector 48. Once inside the house, he headed straight to his almirah, took out his dressing gown, sat on the edge of his bed, removed his black shoes and socks, loosened his tie, and went straight to his bathroom for a warm shower. All lights in the bathroom were switched on. It would take another 15 minutes for the water to warm. Next, he looked for his toothbrush. He was dead tired and wanted nothing more than a relaxing bath and jump straight to his bed.

The mirror reflected a person with a bit longish face and intense eyes. He had an overgrowth of facial hair. Apparently, he had not shaved that day. His eyes were a bit reddish and dreamy. He had his glasses on. The ovoid frame and black titanium gave a nice contrast to his fair complexion. Wiping his full mango lips dry after brushing, he began preparing for his bath.

He switched on his home theater. The violin music in a soft tone echoed around him. Before sinking into his Jacuzzi, he turned again to look at his reflection. He was not too muscular. He was lean with nice and strong muscles.

His mobile had died around evening. From his Jacuzzi, he picked up his phone to activate voice mails. Even in the mobile age, Ihit allowed select clients, special ones, the right to reach him 24/7. Others had to be content with their work phone. He would call them back if he felt it was necessary.

The first call was from Book Corner. The books he had ordered were dispatched, and they would reach him the next day. A smile crossed his lips. He loved reading and has always managed to squeeze in some time to read something daily. After that, there were some unimportant calls. Then there were calls from Dr. Divyansh and Aunt Bijlee. He turned off the shower to listen more intently. In every call, Dr. Divyansh seemed more desperate than the previous one. He needed Ihit to represent Shay.

Ihit nodded, raised his eyebrow, and again a faint smile crossed his lips. His intuition was right about the Vats family reaching him to bail Shay out. He had briefly met the Vats family during Abby's funeral. During the funeral, Dr. Divyansh was looking for a chance to ask about Abby's will. Ihit has been appointed by Abby as her legal counsel. If Abby had a will, then Ihit would be the one who would have drafted it and would execute it. Dr. Divyansh tried to pry some information from Ihit at Abby's funeral. But Ihit declined, stating it was not the appropriate time or place. He had been following Abby's case. If police treated it as murder and filed a charge against any Vats, he would be called to represent him or her. They knew how excellent he was.

In the past, whenever Abby or anybody in the family needed legal counsel or action, Ihit was called. Abby trusted him. Now that Abby was no more, he would be their natural choice if any trouble fell on any of them.

Innocent or guilty, Ihit never judged a case. Masses in his circle disapproved of his approach, labeling it as dishonesty toward the goal of justice. For Ihit, there was nothing dishonest about it. He sincerely defended his clients. He had three rules:

1. Win the case
2. Never convict an innocent
3. Everything else is a fair game

In his heart, he was clear. He believed in whatever he did. His belief gave him sound sleep at night. However, he would not hesitate to destroy relationships or lives if it got him a favorable judgment. A man with almost no friends, his work was his obsession.

Stretching full length in his spacious double bed with a starched white sheet and four rectangular pillows, he called up Vats house. It was half past one, and the phone was picked up by anxious Dr. Divyansh in just about 2 rings.

"Hello"

"Hi, This is Ihit. I received …"

"Ihit! Please come over. Shay is arrested. I don't want him to spend …."

"Hold on, Dr. Divyansh. Don't panic. I am in the city and will meet you in the morning."

"Morning! Shay will be tortured the entire night."

"Believe me, Dr. Divyansh, nothing can be done at this hour. But, when the court opens, I will get bail and be asssured of one thing; I will do anything and everything to help him. Now please give me the details. When was he arrested?"

"Evening"

"Did he confess?"

"How can he? Shay is not a killer. He can't kill."

"Dr. Divyansh, Please, let's not get emotional. It is between you and me. We are covered by Advocate and client confidentiality and privilege, speak freely. Did he or did he not?"

"Not sure…. What were you talking about …?"

"Confession"

"Oh, Confession. No, he has not confessed yet."

"Ask him not to speak a word. Not without my presence there."

That was all Ihit wanted at that moment. He knew that; the police would not resort to third-degree or even second-degree within 24 hours. Shay would be safe in a lock-up. He turned off all lights and went to sleep.

It was dark, and rain was about to break loose. Ihit felt a presence. Slowly, he opened his eyes. It was a girl who was sitting beside him. Slowly, he opened his eyes. He switched on the lights. She was fair and slim with dark hair and big deep dark eyes. Her head was slightly bent down. Her face reflected her thoughts. She was sad. Ihit lifted her face and whispered, "I am sorry, Abby. I had to." A drop of tears rolled down his face.

Next thing Ihit knew that his face was wet. He woke with heavy perspiration. He could hear the torrential rains above his AC, humming at 18 degrees centigrade. Catching his breath, he looked around. Things were undisturbed. It was just a dream, a strange one.

Was Abby restless? Was there something that she wanted Ihit to do? Should he leave the case for good?

All through the night, Ihit kept on thinking about Abby. It was still night. He could see the outlines of trees on his lawn in the white light of the streetlamp struggling through the rain. He sat, closing his eyes, recalling his first meeting with Abby.

Ihit was dealing with a property case, Siddharth Vats Vs. Vivaan Khatri. The case kept on dragging for 4 years. Shabbir Amin, the opposition counsel, gave Ihit a tough time. Then Siddharth met with an accident, and after nearly six months, he passed away. Cena Cosmica fell in hands of a naïve girl, Abhishikta Vats. Maybe that was the reason Shabbir Amin lost the zeal to fight. Ihit was almost handed a gift-wrapped win. Ihit did not bother with hows as long as he won. He went home to find a surprise. A cake was waiting on his table with words, "Congratulations! What next." There was also a bouquet of flowers. The sender did not leave a name, barring a contact number.

Causally, he dialed the number. A soft female voice was on the erstwhile side. The voice has sweetness and a shielded authority, a combination that demands respect. It had been a while since they had this conversation, but he could remember every word.

"Hello, I am Ihit. Thanks for ……"

"You want to know who I am. Truthfully, I am your admirer. I admire the way you handle your cases. Your victory has given me hope. I am fixed in a similar condition. A piece of land was sold to two parties, and the case has been running for 4 years. Isn't it a nice coincidence? I have lost the case; now I want it to be won by you."

"Ma'am, I have a policy of not taking cases over the phone calls. I have to review the documents."

"I am not asking you now to take up this case. I am asking if such a case existed, can it be won? Can you win such a case?"

"Hypothetically, yes, I have won one of such cases. So, yes, I can."

"Then, pleasure talking to you. I hope you are free. I

will be in your chamber in the next 15 minutes," and the line went dead.

There was something mystifying yet romantic about the call. Ihit could not help thinking about the lady who spoke a minute ago. He was unaware of when he had started creating her image in his mind. Whatever the case, his center of interest was the unidentified caller on her way to meet him. He felt as if he was on a blind date.

A limo halted, and a beautiful lady came forward to meet him. "I am AV, owner of Cena Cosmica... I want you to handle my case against Vivaan Khatri."

The introduction impressed him. His visitor, AV, was an intelligent lady. She was one of the few who managed to surprise Ihit. But nevertheless, Ihit maintained his poker face and said.

"I hope you know I represented Vivaan Khatri."

"It was in the past. I have collected all information. You are not under any contractual obligation with Mr. Khatri after this case. You are not a representative of the legal group of Gourmet. You were just called for this case on a trial basis. Now that you have won the case, you can certainly take up my case."

He was impressed by this young woman who had taken the time to collect all the pertinent information to present her case. Smiling, grabbed a plastic fork out from his drawer. He had a habit of dumping extra forks and condominiums in his drawer that had his personal effects. He cut a slice of the cake, offered one portion to the guest, picked the wafer, loaded it with the cream, topped a cherry on it, and started nibbling it.

"True, you have done your homework well. What makes you think that I will take up your case?"

"Not for money, No. Mr. Ihit, you don't care much about money. Neither fringe benefits would interest you. Though nobody could match our offer, it will not tempt you to accept mine. However, you will accept my case because you would meet your match. It would be like representing against yourself, and it'll be a challenge."

"Challenge?"

"Yes, Mr. Ihit, it is easy to defeat your opponents but not easy to fight and win against oneself. This is a kind of challenge that many people will not accept. Something burns you. This fire drives you to take up hopelessly impossible cases."

"But what about loyalty? I stood for one, and now I would stand against them!" Lastly, Ihit teased her with a question on ethics and morality.

Would Ms. AV flinch? How driven was she? Have I met my match?

"You have answered the question. You stood for your clients. When you did, you gave them your loyalty. Now you are not standing for them. You may or may not take my case, but till date, you have never let your emotions mix with your professional life. So don't do it now. The best part is you are not an active advocate in this case. I will be recruiting you as my legal advisor. You know the difference Ihit, don't you? You would be a legal advisor for AV and not an advocate fighting this case. Shabbir will continue to fight in the court, but you will drive the case to victory through him."

Abby was leading him, and he was persuaded and swayed under her charm. Her argument was convincing. She was right, and she came there prepared. She had collected all information about him. It would undeniably be interesting to work with her. The deal was set, and all legal fine prints discussed that would not incriminate Ihit for taking up ex-opponent's case. When she was about to leave when Ihit stopped her with a question,

"Just a question, Ms. AV, was your advocate going soft also part of the plan to win me to your side."

She said nothing but smiled sweetly and left. A smile had answered all Ihit's questions.

"Shit! What a girl! She took such a risk. Shows the confidence she has in herself. I would love to work with her", he murmured aloud.

The first meeting was still livid in his mind. Today sitting on the edge of his bed, he could almost smell the perfume Abby was wearing that day. Ihit took a deep breath. Dawn was breaking. He poured a liberal amount of bourbon, quaffed it, and crept into his bed to catch sleep.

The following day before going to the court, Ihit went to Vats' house to collect all information they had shared with the police. Then he went to the police station. For the next 45 minutes, Ihit and Shay talked.

Getting bail on a murder charge is a bit difficult. The public prosecutor argued that Shay was a flight risk. Ihit argued that Shay has the means but neither inclination nor incentive to flee the charges as he has much to lose if he does so. After half an hour or so of arguments between the public prosecutor and Ihit, Shay was granted bail with a hefty bail bond. The date for the first hearing was in three months.

The Hearing

The first hearing in State vs. Shay Vats case was in March fourth week. For those three months, Ihit worked day and night on the case. He had worked on each link with all the witnesses and Shay. Sooner than later, the day for the first hearing arrived, and the public prosecutor made the opening statement.

He started, "My Lord, the person in front of you is not as innocent as he looks. Neither is he a nice person nor is he a decent citizen. He…"

"Objection, my Lord! Improper character evidence.", Ihit interrupted.

The objection was sustained. The public prosecutor apologized and continued,

"Mr. Shay Vats is accused of murdering Ms. Abhishikta Vats, his cousin. The case is simple and clear. Mr. Shay loves Ms. Mahira, Ms. Abhishikta's friend. But for some reason, she objected to the love between the young couple. She gave Shay a simple option, walk away from the Vats' riches and win his lady love. Shay had sinister plans; he was not ready to leave easy life. He was never on any job and lived life king-size. Shay could not live without money. Money for his red Ferrari, his quarterly trip to Goa and Nepal for gambling, and club membership of the top best clubs in the city. Money for hand-stitched shoes and customized suits. Money that Mr. Shay loves to waste. The money Shay never earned.

What he loves is getting money without any hard work. The accused became desperate when told that he would leave Mahira or be on the roads. He wanted both, but he knew what stuff his cousin was made of. She was stubborn. If she made up her mind about anything, she would not budge from it. The obvious option for Mr. Shay was to remove her from the equation. Kill her!"

"Objection. Speculation."

"Sustained."

"Sorry, my Lord. We have proofs and witnesses who saw Shay attempting to physically harm her. Not once. We will try to prove that Shay tried to kill her cousin twice in the day and failed. But, regrettably, the third attempt was successful."

Shay looked nervous, and so did Dr. Divyansh. Nevertheless, the public prosecutor was building up a compelling story.

"He crept into the farmhouse around 9:00 to 9:30 pm and mixed Liquid Ecstasy in her juice. As usual, she took her food around 10:30 to 10:40 pm, and as per the autopsy report, she took her juice around the same time. The next morning, she was found dead. The caretaker of the farmhouse will testify that he had attempted on her life. His fingerprints are also submitted as evidence. Therefore, there is enough evidence against the accused. And we will be pleading for the highest kind of punishment for the cold-blooded killer."

"It was a nice story. My friend here is hell-bent on proving an innocent man guilty. The story is baseless; my client is innocent as Ms. Abhishikta Vats, also known as Abby, had committed suicide.", was Ihit's short opening statement.

The whole courtroom was buzzing. It was an unexpected turn. Inspector Jai, who was present in the court, replayed the entire investigation sequence in his mind to be double sure that it definitely was not a suicide.

Did he miss anything? He hoped not, *or else the press would have a field day at his expense.*

"So, advocate Ihit, if this is a suicide, where is the suicide note?"

"If this is a murder, where is the eyewitness? Do you have any non-circumstantial proof?"

The public prosecutor called the first witness, Irina, for questioning. She was asked to share her information on the relationship between the cousins.

Irina said, "Shay and AV did have some differences in opinion."

The public prosecutor asked, "What kind of differences?"

"About everything, from the value of money to the relationship."

"Is it true that Ms. Vats opposed the relationship between Shay and Mahira?"

"AV did not approve of his relationship with Mahira."

"Why so?"

"I have no idea."

"Did he abide by her decision?"

"No, it resulted in some heated arguments."

"Did he threaten her?"

Irina thought for some minutes, analyzing her position in the job, and with much confidence, said, "No, I don't think so."

Irina never had Shay in her book of trusted people, but when it came to the delicate position in the job she was in, she thought not to ruin her chances by going against the family.

Ihit had declined his turn to cross-question Irina, saying he would do it later. The next witness was Neer. He was the public prosecutor's star witness.

"Did Mr. Shay Vats go to the farmhouse on the night of 31st Dec?"

"Evening"

"Ms. Abhishikta Vats was going away. Did Shay go to bid her goodbye?"

"No, to ask her to change her decision about him, Shay Sahib and Mahira Madam."

"It must be a friendly family discussion?"

"No, Abby Ma'am kept her cool, but Shay Sahib kept shouting and abusing her and, at times, pleading."

"Did he threaten to kill her?"

"While he was leaving, he did murmur that he would kill anybody who would stand between him and Mahira."

"Did he try to kill her?"

"Twice. Once, when Ma'am opened the door, he nearly strangled her. The second time, she was nearly killed when he threw a heavy brass vase at her. It missed her by some inches."

"That is all, Neer. Your witness Mr. Ihit."

It was time for Ihit to cross-question Neer.

"Neer, when did you last see Abby?"

"10 minutes after Shay Sahib left. She called and gave me a day off for the entire evening on the 31st to enjoy."

"Was she frightened or sad?"

"She was angry when Shay was there. But, after that, when she called me, she was relaxed. She seemed to be happy."

"Point to be noted, My Lord. She had no trace of fear for Shay; not considering Shay as a threat. If Ms. Abhishikta Vats had the slightest apprehension, she would have taken several precautions. She would never be alone. It evidently shows that whatever happened between Shay and her was not serious. Just a family squabble. Which family does not have squabbles? She wanted to be alone on 31st Dec night. Why? Maybe she had already made up her mind to commit suicide?"

The court was adjourned for the day. Some more hearing passed. Then Shay was called for questioning.

"Well, Mr. Shay Vats," the public prosecutor started, "Ms. Abhshikta Vats was your cousin. Did you two get along well?"

"We had our differences; just as families have."

"Other families do not have murders."

"Objection! Badgering the witness."

"Apologies. Strike that off."

"It is unfortunate ... whatever happened to Abby. I am sorry for her."

"So, Mr. Shay, you have no hard feelings about your cousin?"

"As I said earlier, we had our problems, but we would have sorted it out eventually."

"You were confident that things would be sorted out."

"Yes."

"No! You are a liar. You were convinced that nothing of that sort would happen, which drove you to desperation. You planned to kill her."

"No! It is a lie."

"Every word of it is true. You started a cold-blooded murder plan when you said, 'I'll kill everybody who stands between Mahira and me?' And you did it. You killed the one who stood between you two."

"I never meant it. It means nothing. It was a sort of thing one says in a fit of anger."

"You agree you were angry, outraged?"

"Objection, leading the witness," Ihit objected.

"Over-ruled," the Judge said, "I'll let the accused continue."

"I love Mahira. I love her more than my life. She is the one. Don't you understand what it means? Even then, I can never kill anyone, let alone Abby, who was family."

"You tried twice, as per our eyewitness, in a day."

"It was my frustration."

"In frustration, you can kill."

"No! Frustration can lead me to express my anger, but a cold-blood murder is impossible. Truthfully, I am a coward enough to commit such an act."

"You were present there. First, you had tried to strangle Ms. AV, then you threw a vase at your cousin to kill her. You can't deny your presence there. We do have your fingerprints."

"I am not denying my presence. Ask the fingerprints to give you the time when I was there."

The court roared into a peal of laughter, and the public prosecutor continued after a short pause, "By the way, where are you between 9:00pm to 1:30am?"

"No! I was not there if that is what you want to ask?"

"Can you prove it?"

Shay kept mum. *I can never have Mahira find out that after the fight with Abby, I was in a bar, drinking till midnight, and was with an escort from Mall Road in a hotel.*

Now it was Ihit's turn for a counter-argument.

"My Lord, I have been thinking from the killer's point of view. Hypothetically, assume for the sake of argument that Shay is a killer. According to the public prosecutor, Shay tried to kill her twice that evening but failed. Then Shay creeps in at night, and instead of killing her in an easy conventional manner, he chooses to kill her by using an overdose of liquid Ecstasy. Well! So far, so good. Shay spikes her drink. Then he waits, and she comes in and drinks it. Then he waits till Ms. AV dies. Then Shay goes to the farmhouse. He removes all the fingerprints from all the places except the two places, the vase and the doorknob. Why? Would it not be easier to rub the fingerprint out from those two places too? Is it not too illogical? There is nothing to indicate that this is a crime of passion. Killing someone for love would likely be a crime of passion than pre-meditated murder. I fail to see any evidence pointing towards the crime of passion."

"My friend, the public prosecutor insists that Shay has killed Ms. AV in anger. Such murder would be like a crime of passion and would not have such detailed planning and careless miss. Imagine Shay wipes all traces of fingerprints and leaves out the two places that had proof of his anger."

"One of the motives for this so-called murder was that Shay would benefit greatly from her death. There are others, too, who would gain more from her death. Take an example of a businessman called Vivaan Khatri. He would gain the most from Ms. AV's death. Can we accuse him of her death? Is this not proper? Whatever evidence my friend has got is circumstantial. Everything is based on assumptions. On assumptions only, I can prove that my client is innocent."

The Judgement

The next witness that Ihit called was Inspector Jai.

"Officer, can you throw some light as to why you concluded this as murder?"

"There was strong evidence regarding motive, fingerprints, and accessibility. Shay had threatened Ms. Abhishikta twice. He had easy access to meth, which was used to kill her, and he could have clandenstinely mixed it with her drinks. No forced entry; suggests that the perp was someone she knew and trusted. In all this, the person who would fit the bill is Shay."

"Why did you say that Shay has easy access to meth?"

"Shay's father, Dr. Divyansh, has a lab in the same house. I found the same potion in his lab."

"Did Ms. AV live in the same house?"

"To my knowledge, yes."

"She could also have the easy access to the chemical?"

"I guess so," Jai added non-confidently.

"Invariable guess that you made about Shay. Anyway, let's move to the next question, do you have eyewitness?"

"Yes, Neer, who saw Shay attack Ms. AV twice."

"Is this not strange? Shay attacks Ms. AV twice, in presence of a witness; and then walks away to return and poison the juice. If he wanted, he would have done it."

"Calls for Speculation," interjected the public prosecutor.

"Sustained.", ruled the judge.

"Sorry, My Lord," Ihit continued, "Officer Jai, it is established that Neer left the farmhouse at 5:00pm instead of 4:00pm. Murder or suicide happened around 9:30pm. Would it be possible that Ms. AV went somewhere? She either had the drugs or carried them home to use?"

"We do not have any CCTV in the farmhouse or in that area to confirm Abby going out of the farmhouse."

"Can you rule it out as impossible?"

"I don't understand where my friend, Mr. Defense Attorney, is going with this theory," a hassled public prosecutor demanded.

"I am saying that it is not without a reasonable doubt that anybody here can say it was not a suicide. But, with so much evidence that is circumstantial and doubtful, Ms. AV's death could be a suicide. So how did police conclude it was a murder?"

"Was there a question for me?" Jai asked

"I keep wondering why her death was probed as a murder and not ruled a suicide."

"We had motives. We had a witness who placed the accused at the crime scene. So, deriving it further was a logical conclusion."

"Did Ms. AV drink?"

"There was alcohol in her stomach and bloodstream as per the autopsy report."

"My Lord, we have submitted exhibit J, which testifies that Ms. AV never used to drink. None of her people had ever seen her drink. The question is, then, how could alcohol come into her blood? There was no sign of forcible entry to her place. Nobody forced her to drink alcohol. She must have had it herself, don't you think so, Officer?"

"Maybe."

"Did you find any of Ms. AV's fingerprints in any of the bottles of alcohol in her farmhouse's bar?"

"No."

"Did you even dust the prints or look at any of the bottles as evidence?"

"The chemical was found in the glass containing juice. Therefore, eliminating the need to find another source of the drugs."

"Did it not appear strange that a person who does not drink has alcohol in her blood? What triggered it?"

"How would I know that? I assumed it was New Year's Eve and Ms. AV had some drinks. It isn't a crime to start drinking on a new year eve."

"It was your assumption, which is not proven by any evidence. All evidence pointed out that Ms. AV did not drink. So, what happened? There is absence of physical evidence suggesting someone forced her. Instead, she consumed alcohol for the first time. Why?"

"Heresy," chimed the public prosecutor.

"I am humbly trying to establish the state of mind of Ms. AV. That would prove that suicide is not beyond the reasonable doubt." Ihit defended.

"Overruled." was the judge's reaction.

"I would like to bring forth witnesses who can shed more light on Ms. AV's state of mind. Do I have permission to cross-examine Ms. Irina?"

On the call, Irina confidently walked up to the witness stand.

"Ms. Irina, thanks for coming to the court again. Can you shed some light on the nature and behavior of Ms. Abhishikta Vats?"

"She was gentle but firm when it came to discipline. Workaholic, dedicated, and had a passion for reaching the top."

"Is it an abnormal behavior?"

"No! She was by any defination, normal. A bit sensitive but normal."

"How can you say that?"

"Whenever she was alone, she used to be lost in some thoughts. One of our waiters slipped and fell; he had damaged his spinal cord paralyzing him from the waist down. The company was not supposed to pay for the complete treatment as the accident happened in his home after duty hours. AV helped him with the entire treatment and is still paying his monthly salary from her personal account. She was a compassionate person."

"How were her last few months?"

"She was too disturbed. Abby did not confide in me. She took ages to open up and confide her problem with anybody. She was utterly detached. Suddenly, she appeared incredibly happy, a week or two before this incident."

"Thanks, Irina, you may go," Ihit addressed the Judge, "My Lord, I would like to throw a light on Ms. AV's mental condition. I would like to call Dr. Rubina Ahmed, Assistant HOD of Psychology, State Medical College."

"Dr. Ahmed, you heard statements about Ms. Abhishikta. I have already shared court transcripts about the victim with you. Would you please share about her mental condition?"

"It is obvious; Ms. Abhishikta lived under considerable stress. She projected herself to be stern. She was disciplined and dedicated. But the hidden side of her personality was diagrammatically opposite. She was soft, helpful, and to a large extent, vulnerable. It was difficult. Her sternness did not allow her to reach out to others in need, but she wanted to reach out to them. She contained all her feelings within herself. In reality, she perhaps needed somebody to share her pain. Everybody has a saturation point, a limit. When that limit is crossed, either person emerges stronger or crumbles down."

"Is it possible that such a person, who is also so successful, can commit suicide?"

"Have you not followed the history of celebrity

suicides? Success or money has nothing to do with inner peace or happiness. It is different. Everybody has a distinctive approach, priorities, and destination in life, along with their desires and wants. So maybe success was not something she longed for."

"Do you think Ms. AV could have committed suicide?"

"It is difficult to say, but the preceding few days, as described, seem to indicate something like that."

"Point to be noted is that Ms. Abhishikta could have committed suicide. Your turn Mr. Public Prosecutor."

"Thanks, Advocate Ihit! Now Dr. Ahmed, can you please take a guess as to why anybody would die on the day she has planned to go to travel? And why in such an unconventional manner? It is easier to procure sleeping pills, but why liquid Ecstasy? Meth, which is not readily available? Why would someone commit suicide with full makeup and music in a designer dress? Is it not too weird?"

"Some people find the notion of death profoundly romantic. Others want to go with glory. For some, it is a journey to another life, and they want to go prepared. Now to answer the question, why die with full makeup on…. It might be possible that she looked at death as her lover who would relieve her from all the pain of this real world; a defense mechanism of the mind. It is nothing but an unproductive fantasy to escape from the frustration of imbalance. She wanted to welcome death and slip into unknown woods with him. She would have been a romantic person. The mind is complex; it can also take practicality, like death, as a hero or a savior.

Regarding why just before travel? It can be a stressor that triggered her suicide."

Ihit was on a roll. Every minute he spoke, more doubts were cast on treating the case as a suicide. Then, he called his final witness for the day.

"My Lord, till now, I have lined up evidence strongly suggesting that Ms. AV could have committed suicide. My concluding witness today will prove that Ms. AV had easy access to the lab. She could have taken the meth from there."

Ihit continued with his questioning once Dr. Divyansh was in the witness box.

"Dr. Vats, did Ms. AV know about your lab?"

"The lab was on Abby's property. She was extremely particular about cataloging them. Making certain that no chemical was not banned or unapproved. She hired junior scientists as a freelancer every month to audit and catalog. As a result, she knew most of the chemicals there."

"Is there a possibility that Ms. AV would have known that methylenedioxymethamphetamine could be taken as a recreational drug or a bit more could be taken for suicide?"

"Abby knew the nature of most of the chemicals. During the catalog and audit process, she asked voluminous questions. If she discovered that Methylenedioxymethamphetamine could be used, she could have come to the lab at any time and taken it. She had free access to it."

No further questions were asked. The court was adjourned. Two more hearings happened, from Abby's father's will to her obsession with work were all discussed, and all witnesses were questioned and re-examined. The date of the final hearing came. The public prosecutor started with the closing arguments on the said date, "My Lord! My friend Advocate Ihit Basu still cannot prove that Shay was not there. He had the motive and accessibility. He seized the opportunity and killed her. We had produced a witness who testified about the violent nature of the accused."

"Yes, I could not prove that Shay Vats is not a killer. But neither has the State proved beyond a reasonable doubt that Shay Vats is a killer. True, his fingerprints were found, and my client has not denied his argument with her cousin. It was a family squabble. However, the police could not find any proof that Shay poisoned his cousin. There were no fingerprints or credible witnesses there. Both witnesses testified of differences, but where was the eyewitness who saw the crime? We have not ruled out suicide either. Can anybody, without a reasonable doubt, say it was Shay who killed his cousin? I don't think so. There are no proofs to place my client at the crime scene during the time of the crime. My job here was to protect the life of this innocent man. Shay appeared guilty because of the complex circumstances. There is no sign of forced entry except the circumstantial evidence against Shay. It's even doubtful if it was a murder. It could be suicide, as Dr. Ahmed said."

After a discussion with the jury, the decision was out.

"During the course of the argument, the public prosecutor produced evidence that Shay was in the farmhouse. On the question of motive, reasonable doubt was created on the motives of Dr. Divyash and Bijlee Vats. Both had a lot to gain from Ms. Abhishikta's death. I could have hoped that the police had done a wholesome job. The police did not implicate them and had ruled them out as suspects except for Shay. The accused has not denied his presence in the farmhouse nor the heated argument. Like the accused, the others, her family members, her friends and her competition had the motive and means to eliminate her. Agreed, Shay had easy access to his father's lab and could have gotten the potion Liquid Ecstasy. So did the deceased. The defendant's advocate has established that Ms. Vats had the basic knowledge of the presence of meth in her uncle's lab. In that case, her death could be suicide. The public prosecutor could not produce evidence that was not circumstantial to pass a guilty verdict without a reasonable doubt. I wished the case could have been handled a bit better. Some questions could not be answered, raising reasonable doubt. On that basis, I find Mr. Shay Vats not guilty by virtue of reasonable doubt. The case is dismissed."

Jai never had imagined how dramatically the case got away from him. Instead of being a career builder, it proved a disaster. Narender would make certain to keep rubbing salt into his injury.

Once the verdict was out, Ihit was mobbed by the press. The drama in the courtroom had caught media attention. Ihit had given the case a perplexing twist. Slowly, Abby had evolved from a focused businesswoman to an enigma. The city swiftly realized that they had an opportunity to decipher the complexity of Abby and pass on a verdict themselves. Ihit's efforts in court had raised the question of the nature of Abby's death. Was it a murder or a suicide? The city was talking about this perplexing case of an enigma.

Part – II: Transcended & Home Truth

Hello C

Back home, Ihit went straight to his private den. It was a smaller room compared to the other rooms, measuring around 15ft by 15 ft. Towards the west was a study table with a simple steel table lamp and a pen set. Adjacent to the table was a revolving shelf. On the eastern side was a hearth. The hearth was cold. Spring was in the city; there wasn't any need for the fire. Ihit went to the shelf, picked up a pile of diaries, and took it to his study table. He picked up the first diary from the stack.

The diary was seven years old. The first entry was on 30th September; all the pages before this date were blank.

7 years ago || Abby's age – 16 years

30th September

Today is my 16th birthday. If people are to be trusted, I am entering an incredible year of my life. This year I am told, would be the year of foolishness and gaining wisdom. Several years from today, when I am old, sitting on my rocking chair looking outside through the glass window to the winder bloom, how much I would laugh and cry reading these entries.

I am Abby, Abhishikta Vats.

What should I call you? You are my confidante. I shall address you as Confiada. Or Should I call you C?

Dear C,

This is our first meeting.

It was Abby's diary. Emotions choked his throat, and Ihit paused to catch his breath. The image of Abby came alive. She was bit more than a client. With her death, Ihit had lost a close friend. Moist eyes, ragged breath, he continued reading.

Let me introduce you to the most critical person in my world. It is my Papa. I have the best father anybody could have asked for. I agree we have lesser time to spend together, but whatever time Papa takes out to be with me, he does not let anything bother us then. I am okay with lesser quantity when it comes to time. I get the best quality one.

My life is a dream. I do fine in my studies and am not pushed to be in the top 1% of the class. Next year, I will be in some college. There is a matter of choosing my stream. That requires some planning; otherwise, I don't have to strictly plan for the future. Unlike my friends, I am under no pressure to hunt for a job and support the family. We are well-off, rich, but it has never got to my Papa's head. He still insists on saving, not wasting, not being extravagant, and living modestly. Of course, the one luxurious thing in our lives is Cena Cosmica. Cena Cosmica, our theme restaurant. Papa is working hard to make it a brand, a go-to hub. And it is all for me, to get my future safe. Though it isn't needed, we have enough to survive two lifetimes. Papa says that somehow lifestyle grows to the extent of your riches, and rolling back is difficult. He has never put a restraint on my spending, or he never had to.

Why should I concern myself with all these grueling topics of finance? Papa is there to handle it for me. He is making definite of my stable future. My job here is to enjoy life before I eventually take up the responsibilities of Cena Cosmica. And that my friend, is after many years.

Yes, I miss Mom. Papa seldom speaks about her. It is okay. Everyone deals with loss and grief in their own way. He prefers to be silent; I, like to talk. I share my feelings with my friends and, from now on, you. Life is to be enjoyed. I don't believe in keeping emotions bottled up. You and I would share a lot.

Until I return to you, C, keep smiling and laughing. The world is such a lovely place.

Luv, Abby

Ihit skipped some more pages.

24th November

Dear C,

The winter has set in.

The air is nippier though the sky is clear and often star-studded. Such a setting for love. Not surprisingly, people are falling in love. Kyra has fallen for Manav. I fail to see what she sees in that guy! He has failed in his class twice! He is gawky and definitely, clout compared to the debate champion. Well, love is blind.

I don't like him, but Kyra's eyes light up with a crazy, stupid and dreamy look at the mention of his name. But she does think the world of him. Maybe, it is just a phase. Hope it ends soon. Don't like my friends to be stupid.

That's all for now, Abby.

30th November

Dear C,

I am elated! I have joined a dance class. I have opted for all three western dance forms offered in the institute. They will teach us everything, from sexy salsa to the elegant ballroom dance to naughty tango.

My heart races when I dance. I don't remember feeling anything better. I float when I dance; the surroundings blur, I feel a sweet taste on my lips, and my breath is inebriated.

I am so thrilled. There are 10 students in my class, and there are 3 who have opted for all the dance forms. Classes will begin from 7th of next month.

I know, what you are thinking, C. This is my final undergrad year; how can I spend so much time dancing? Most of my friends are taking coaching classes to crack MBA. I don't have to do that. In one instance, Papa suggested that. Spending time in his office with him would be a worthier education than MBA to manage Cena Cosmica. I have ample time for that. Meanwhile, I would prefer to live and enjoy life doing what I like doing, dancing.

I can almost not sit down and write.

Luv, Abby.

3rd December (Actually, it is 4th December)

Dear C,

I am shivering, and my pulse is elevated. It's precisely 2:28 am. I will have a cup of coffee to ward off any sleep that may come in. I don't want to sleep. The nightmare would come back to me if I closed my eyes. It began like a movie and ended with a nightmare.

The sky was in its deepest blue shade. I was standing in the middle of some kind of flower garden. There were countless flowers in all directions extending to the horizon. The soft sun's warmth was on my skin in contrast to the balmy, moist wind from neighboring fields where it had perhaps rained heavily at night.

I can vividly recall the fragrances floating in the air. I was standing there with my face towards the sky and my eyes closed. I wanted to feel everything. Then I heard somebody calling out my name. It seemed to echo from every direction.

I was smiling and trying to find the owner of the voice. I was looking everywhere. In a moment, I found myself running. I was running perilously from someone to save my life.

I did not see any face, but I could feel the chase all along.

It seems pretty silly to be frightened of a nightmare after waking up. But this was no dream like I had ever seen. It was different. I can never explain the feeling of knowing your life could slip away at any moment. It was frightening.

I hope, Dear C, I have not frightened you as well.

Frightened, Abby

Ihit could not help smiling. He was sharing a romantic moment with a sixteen-year-old version of her friend. How unlike was this Abby from the one everyone knew? This girl was naïve, and the Abby he met first knew the world's ways. A lot would have happened in a short span of six years. A sigh escaped his lips, and he continued reading.

7th December

Dear C,

Somehow, I know someone is looking out for me. I thought I would miss a term. We were 5 students in the dance class. We have a lottery to choose the partner for the next 2 months. Since I was without a partner, I thought I had to wait till the next group got admitted, but my terrific luck. Sir's assistant would be my partner! I would surely learn more. I am happy, and I have to work harder too.

Psssst: He is handsome too!

Happy, Abby.

31st December

Dear C,

This year since my birthday, I have started writing to you, C. I feel splendid sharing these intimate thoughts with you.

This is the sweet 16th year of my life. Till now, everything has been outstanding; it was a smashing year. I have started my dance class. Father seems a slightly more worried and is undoubtedly busier.

I am looking forward to another terrific year.

Optimistic, Abby

The diary was over; Ihit picked up the next one. It was with a brown leather jacket with golden clips in 2 corners. The first page was colored with assorted colors with the sfumato effect. Cursive handwriting in black ink gave it an exquisite look.

---

6 years ago || Abby's age – 17 years

1st January

Dearest C,

Happy New Year!!!

I have colored the first page with the colors of joy and hope. I wish the whole year goes in this way.

Nothing more to write except I had class today, which was a sort of party. I had a wonderful time. Some students from different institutes were also invited.

I danced all the time. I am dead tired, ready to dance again, but in my dreams.

Bye with hugs, Abby.

26th February

Dear C,

Hold me tight, for today has been such a depressing day. I feel like drowning in a sea of heaviness.

God! Is it happening? My neighbor Falak, she is no more. I still remember her as a bride barely under two years. She was such a joyous person, always smiling.

Somebody threw acid at her when she was on her way home. Police are investigating the matter. Nobody knows who they were? Or why she was attacked. Her husband seems to be upset.

The doctors did everything they could for a week, but she could not pull through.

Falak, Rest in Peace.

Abby.

Ihit was randomly picking pages to read. He was breezing through the intimate details of Abby's life. He could almost feel Abby reading the pages to him.

15th April

Dear C,

Have you ever experienced something you can never explain to others while you understand what you have seen or felt?

A strange thing happened today. I was feeling a negligeably upset; belatedly but the stress of exams, and the anxiety of the cut-off percentage increasing every year, caught up with me.

The infuriating part is that more than half of my class, with a much lesser score, will be admitted without any problem. Thanks to the myopic rules.

To add to the confusion, I can't decide what stream, Arts, Science, or Commerce, to pursue. What do I like? What if I want something today and then don't like it? What are my friends choosing? Several questions!

I felt a gentle grip of a firm hand on my shoulder and a breath on my nape. I turned around; I was alone. Of course, I saw nobody there, but still, I could feel someone in a breath's distance whispering, 'Don't worry, I'll always be with you.'

I wish I could write more, but exam time.

I will come back to you after 3 months.

Feeling fine and assured Abby.

9th August

Dear C,

Kyra and I had a fight. I don't think we'll ever be friends again. She is so possessive and jealous. So happened, Prisha from another school joined the dance class. We instantly struck a rapport. But Kyra did not like it. All because Prisha was Manav's ex. (Remember Manav, the clout, I don't like, and Kyra's boyfriend). Kyra is insecure about Prisha when Prisha plainly does not care for Manav anymore.

I expected more of Kyra.

I don't like this attitude. Just because Kyra is my best friend, she can't make all the decisions for me. I don't need her to tell me who should be my friend. She is not my mom! It is just sick.

Yours, Abby.

18th October

Dear C,

I thought of writing, but my mood changed. I feel like walking up the terrace and nap under the stars.

Luv, Abby.

31st December

Another year has come to an end. The main points:

Falak is no more. She died due to an acid attack. Nobody knows why it was so and who did it. My sort of best friend Kyra and I are no more friends. Never expected Kyra to be so mean and insecure. On the brighter side, I got another friend in Prisha.

Papa is not in the town. We will have a party when he comes back.

Apart from few insignificant incidents, which I am not sure, I will remember after a year or two, this was an uneventful year, Abby.

Another diary had come to an end. So Ihit picked up another five-year-old journal.

5th January

Dearest C,

Why is this happening to me?

Ihit could scantly read; the handwriting was all scrawly. It was distant from Abby's elegant cursive writing. Some words were tear-soaked and were almost unreadable.

Papa is in ICU. Some freak accident has sent him there. The doctors say that I would never hear him speak. He may never see me, never open his eyes. He may never wake up.

Papa had insufficient time for me, but I never complained. He and I both made the best of it. It does not feel right that even that will be snatched away from me. Not like this.

Feeling Helpless, Abby.

Ihit closed his eyes. He could feel Abby crying. This accident changed Abby's life and triggered the events that ultimately ended with her death. Somewhere Abby could feel the ominous tiptoes eager to rob her of her happiness. Why couldn't she think of the hushed footsteps of her death?

Ihit let the feeling sink in as he closed his eyes and sat with her diary for some more time before continuing to read it.

8th January

Dear C,

There is a ray of hope. A feeble light struggling through the dark clouds of desperation and helplessness has landed in my heart. Today at about 2:30 pm, Papa regained his sense.

Three days! Three days after that horrible accident on the highway where his car rammed against a parked truck loaded with iron rods. The driver of the truck escaped unhurt. Destiny or fate, whatever one wishes to call it, played such a dirty trick.

Papa never enjoys driving at night. God knows why he did choose to drive that night. He sent the driver and aimlessly went around the neighborhood for 2 hours. Around 2 am, his car ran into a parked truck carrying iron rods. Although the truck was parked with parking lights on, with no indication of rods emerging from it. My father is paying the price for the carelessness of the truck driver.

When they got him to the hospital, he had lost considerable blood and had an internal hemorrhage. He had a slim chance of survival. He has been fighting so hard for the past three days to be back with me. The doctors are cautiously optimistic. Doctors confirm it as a fair sign for the danger has passed. He had opened his eyes and called out my name. It may be nothing, but still, it has built up the crumbling hope.

Please, Papa, please get well soon. I need you.

I am feeling terribly lonely, come back to me. Please don't go to Mom.

Abby.

15th February

Dear C,

I don't know if father's condition improved or worsen. He does not often slip into a coma, and luckily, he does not remain unconscious for long. But he is not what he used to be. Doctors have confirmed that he is paralyzed, neck down.

He would never walk or sit. He would need help for each and everything. I am so shattered seeing such a self-dependent and proud man be in this state. Papa has taken it gracefully. I have hidden my tears from others, but in you, I am confiding my cherished friend, C; this pain is eating away my life.

Today, Papa said he was going to talk to his lawyer, brother, and sister. I am scared. I do not like this. But he told me; he would discuss something essential with me tomorrow. What would it be?

Tired, Abby.

28th February

Dear C,

Papa's sibling and my cousin are here per my father's wish. Papa seems to be in a hurry to resolve all differences between his siblings. He seems to have forgotten what aunt Bijlee did to my mom when she was alive. Uncle always sided with Aunt Bijlee. So both brother and sister are evil.

Why is my father so blind to Aunt Bijlee's faults?

I remember all the horrible things that happened courtesy of aunt Bijlee and uncle Divyansh. Those I had almost forgotten about them. They were out of sight and out of our lives. But now Papa wants to reconcile with them! I find it hard to forgive them.

Now that they are here, all those memories have come back to haunt me. I tried to look forward and put those things behind me, but I can't forget that Aunt Bijlee was always the cause of my mom's unhappiness. She was the cause of the fight between Papa and Mom. I just don't like her.

Aunt Bijlee would report all trivial matters in such a mischievous way that would result in an ugly verbal duel between Papa and Mom. It continued for years. The evil brother-sister duo was always jealous of my mother. They felt insignificant in front of her, and she never bothered to argue with them. She would keep quiet. Maybe that was her fault. She never stood up for herself. And the bitch of my aunt always twisted the words and projected her as a conniving woman.

That woman tried to poison me against my mom. I did not believe her because I was always with her like my mom's shadow. I had seen her being selfless and speaking well about this woman who was out to destroy her life. She would always say, "Your aunt is not a bad woman. She is childish and short-tempered. Don't forget, she was my friend, and I met your father because of her. So for this act of hers, I can forgive her." I never liked my aunt's eyes. They were small, cunning, and always sparkled with greed.

As a child, my intuitions about her were so correct. However, it took years for my Papa to realize the kind of woman my aunt was.

Fortunately one day, Papa found the truth. No clue how or what he found out. He confronted Aunt Bijlee. Papa guessed that Aunt Bijlee had some hidden agenda. Uncle Divyansh knew that aunt was wrong, but he always stood beside her, no matter what. They were like two peas in a pod.

Papa asked them to leave our house.

Both the siblings left home and went to the bungalow, the ancestral house in another state. Even on Mom's death, all they did was send a condolence message.

I cannot accept them as my family. I am at my wit's end as to why Papa called them when he knows they are just parasites? They are not our family. Our family comprises of two of us. So what is the point of calling these people now?

If Papa wants to patch up with them, I have no problem but do not expect me to love or respect them. They can never be my family.

Angry, Abby.

It was the most extended entry Abby had made. Ihit could feel the rage she felt as she penned down the entries. She was pouring her heart out. Though Aunt Bijlee and Dr. Divyansh were related to her by blood, they were not her family. Instead, they were a set of opportunist bottom feeders who had come back into Abby's life, much against her wishes.

19th March

Dear C,

The hospital is my another address. I spend most of the time with Papa. Uncle stays busy in his lab, and so is Aunt Bijlee in her own schemes. What a support system my father has?

Shay is a great help these days. Rare sweet memories of my relatives are of my adolescent days with Shay. Shay was one of the greatest cheats ever born. Our afternoon games would begin with great promise and always end with a big fight.

We could never hold grudges; we played, ultimately to fight once again. Shay was a sore loser.

After my uncle left home, I had no contact with him. Shay's image as a prankster kid was stuck in my mind. When he came back, I was somewhere expecting to meet my old cousin. I was disappointed to meet a different Shay.

I have no idea what he is now. He is so changed (so am I). We are no longer kids, but he has changed a lot, and I can't put finger on it.

Somehow, I miss those days. I miss my old buddy Shay.

Nostalgic, Abby

Growing Up

5 years ago || *Abby's age – 18 years*

12th April

Dear C,

Winter gave in to Spring. Trees are dressing up for a beautiful phase in life. Life, however, appears the routine for me, with no further improvement in Papa's condition. He keeps moving in and out of ICU. But he has insisted on me joining my classes. Even in this condition, he is so keen on the business.

He has started explaining the work in detail this week. He wants me to join the family business soon. I'm curious if I am cut out for this. At least not now. I am not ready.

Somewhere, I don't have a promising feeling about this. Why is Papa taking all the pain to explain the business to me?

He will get well, and he'll handle it. No hurry. I keep repeating these lines. Still, a feeble voice whispers, "Is it? Do we have as much time as we would like?" Deep inside, a voice tells me to look around and accept the signs that he may not be around.

Few moments I have seen death hovering around. I chose not to listen. Hope my obstinate hope wins.

And now, I am getting ready to help him with his work when he returns.

Determined, Abby

2nd May

Dear C,

Doctors are hiding something. I was involved till Papa regained his senses. Now, he is in charge of his recovery. He is the one who interacts with doctors and makes all the decisions.

Per what doctors have said, there is nothing to worry about. So why is Papa undergoing operations after operations? Why my heart feels something is wrong?

Waiting for things to get better, Abby.

25th May

Dearest C,

It is so easy to give up and so difficult to carry on.

There could be no greater pain than seeing one's father helpless. It is heart-wrenching. Still, it is nothing compared to those battling lifelong confinement in a wheelchair. Yet, my father is fighting it with a smile on his lips. He is my Hero.

That is the mantra of success, continue no matter what to make the next day a superior day. That is how he reached the top; I ought to do this. I'll enjoy business. I am my Papa's daughter.

Preparing, Abby

Ihit poured himself a glass of aged Scotch Whiskey. He needed it. The dreams of a naïve 16-year-old transforming into a strong person dealing with uncertainties in life were overwhelming. He quaffed a large peg and got one more to his reading table.

3rd June

Dear C,

Papa is to have another operation tomorrow. So, we spent the entire day together. He shared something important with me before the procedure.

True, I am no more a child. But, as soon as I entered the threshold of adulthood, fate assured I grew up.

What I learned today is so difficult to process. I can't even write it here. I have sworn secrecy and will honor this promise given to my father. I have discovered something that rips my heart, and I can't share it with anybody. Nobody can know about it.

Gosh! I am stunned. Where do I stand? I am standing on a layer of quicksand, sinking fast. A moment earlier, everything was so real; now, nothing is.

Everything appears like an illusion. So whom do I trust, and to what degree should I trust?

This color of the world, which I wished never existed, is neoteric to me.

I hope he recovers after the operation.

Feeling low, Abby

4th June

Dear C,

Before going to Operation Theatre, he said to me, 'Abby, my Abby darling. I wish I would never have to expose you to the harsh realities of my world so soon. But, lamentably, circumstances have forced me to share this ugliness with you. I have done half of the work. Rest half is left for you. Never commit the mistakes I have made. Try and try your best to achieve what I have lost. I know I can trust you on that front. You are my courageous girl. Fight! This is my blessing.'

Why did it feel like he was saving it to be his ultimate message?

It is over five hours after the operation. Papa has not regained his senses.

Praying there are no complications, Abby.

8th June

Dear C,

Nothing is right! Papa has not yet regained his senses. Worse, all of his organs are failing. The doctors assure that they are doing their best. Some experts have been called. Just do anything, God, take my organs and save him.

I love you, Papa. Please get well soon. Nothing seems assuring without you.

You promised that you would not let tears come to my eyes. You said you would be with me always. These six months are enough. They feel like six fucking years. I can no longer carry on; I am weary and tired. They have changed me a lot. I don't want to change anymore; I want to be your naive little girl again. Papa, please come back to me.

Waiting for you, Papa.

Your's Abby.

13th June

Dear C,

Papa left me all alone in this world, and I hate Papa for this.

I never thought he would break my trust. So what is the difference between him and others? Whom should I trust, and how much?

He had no right to leave without giving me time to prepare for such an eventuality.

I think Aunt Bijlee, uncle, and perhaps even Shay knew about his condition. Why else would those people stay here for so long if they did not sense some profit or material gain?

It is shocking to know that the Doctors had informed him that there was irreparable damage. They had given you 4-6 months. Yet, he kept this information away from me. Why? Why did Papa do this? We shared a lot then. Why did he distance me so much?

I feel so alienated and betrayed. I do not know if the sense of loss or this perfidy hurts more.

I wished he loved me a bit more to fight harder to stay on with me.

At least, now he is with Mom, reunited. I wish them to be happy. But I am all alone now.

Mom, Papa, your Abby is quite lonely and is in a terrible nightmare.

Please wake me up.

It was difficult for Ihit to read.

Writing in black ink was smeared. It was evident that Abby had been crying. It was a changed Abby. The Abby he had seen was more formidable and would never cry. The Abby who poured her heart out to her Confidante, C, was a vulnerable girl dealing with the loss of her single parent.

It was difficult to believe that Abby was once a simple girl who painted one page of her diary with color and another with tears. Ihit could see young Abby laying her head on her friend's lap, crying her heart out till sleep overcame her pain.

Siddharth Vat's death was a big blow to Abby. She was left alone in the world, forced to share her life with people she could neither forget nor forgive.

Ihit wondered, would Abby still be alive had her father been in charge of Cena Cosmica? Ihit sighed as he realized the sequence of events that started with one death inescapably ended with another.

23rd July

Dear C,

I am done with crying. It won't help; it won't get my Papa back. I have wasted enough time. Now I have to go through all the files at the office and keep the chain running.

A tough job, and genuinely, I am scared. But I know I will do it; I can feel it. Let me prioritize.

1st I have to get over this court case with Vivaan Khatri. This advocate, Ihit, is a smart cookie. He knows he cannot win, so he is dragging the case.

Our advocate is not bad, but Ihit Basu is proficient and a sly fox.

I must get him to our side.

Yours, Abby.

A smile crossed his lips. He had no idea Abby was keen to get him to her side long before she met him. It seemed a lifetime ago. Ihit turned some pages.

12th August

Dearest C,

I have collected some information on advocate Ihit. He is much more talented than I had expected. He would be an asset to Cena Cosmica. The problem is he is representing Vivaan Khatri, locked over a property case with us in court. So it will be unethical and wrong to try and win him during this court case.

It will be a challenge to win him to my side. It will be fun. Let us wait and watch.

Abby

Ihit could see the evolution of Abby from a naive, scared girl to a confident woman who enjoyed challenges.

24th September

Dear C,

Again, I had the numinous feeling and heard the intimate voice calling out to me. I seldom talk about it, but I am confident you remember the unseen face and an unknown voice that is an echo of someone who loves me. This time I saw a shadow-like figure but, alas, no face. I wish I could see his face. That feeling still lingers on.

In my garden, I was sleeping on my ease chair under a goldmohur tree. The air was loaded with champak and jasmine odor. It was dusk. Pinkish shades of the shy sun blended un-uniformly under the charm of blue, somewhere blushing a modicum more than required. I was drifting in and out of sleep. Was I indeed asleep? I am still determining. In my dreams, though, I could hear the birds and distant voices.

Strange as it might sound, I was on the corridor of two worlds.

The sound of the evening appeared to be an echo from a distance. I was floating on air. I felt so light. The weariness of the days gone by was gone. Instead, I was refreshed by a shower of invisible rain.

I felt him! I felt his warm breath on my face. He was incredibly close to me and softly whispered, 'Abby'. I opened my eyes to find him standing over me. It was dark enough for me to see his face, but I felt I had known him all my life. At that moment, I did not recognize him; in my heart, I knew he was no stranger. In a hesitant voice, I asked, "Who are you?"

"Don't you know? Your heart knows me. It is me you were waiting for", his voice had a smile. I nodded. Somehow, I knew he was the answer I was seeking.

"What do I call you?"

"You can call me anything you feel like. Truth is that I am the love you seek but will never admit."

My thoughts were rudely interrupted by aunt Bijlee who thought I was dreaming with my eyes open.

Was it a dream? No! I can still feel his warm breath. It can never be a dream. I can still smell the mix of earth, woods, and musk from him.

I will call him Abeer. He is my Abeer.

Your Abby is waiting for you, Abeer.

Feeling her presence in the dead pages of the diary, Ihit tenderly started stroking the pages. He had never seen Abby as beloved, pinning for her lover. After a long time, he turned some pages.

8th October

Dearest C,

Today, Cena Cosmica lost a case to Ihit Basu. I am graeteful, my gamble paid off. Ihit Basu is joining as my legal counselor or advisor to supervise all the legal stuff for me.

No one remembered. It's mom's birthday today. Every year Papa and I used to wish mom together. So guess, this year, Papa wished Mom happy birthday in person.

I continued the tradition Papa and I had made of doing everything she liked on her birthday. I got up early, wore my favorite dress, and distributed food and sweets in orphanages. I also did something extra; I spent my entire afternoon with people in an Old Age Home. They liked it. Time is more precious than money for me, and my company is much more valuable to them. Still, I miss them. I tried to keep myself occupied in something or the other; still, can feel emptiness without them. Can there be some miracle, and they come back?

Come back, please, Abby.

28th November

Dear C,

I am feeling glum today. I know I have a set of targets to achieve; I am working towards it, but still, a deep sense of loneliness prevails.

Aunt Bijlee, uncle, and Shay are staying in the house. It was Papa's wish, so I did not challenge it. Aunt Bijlee is trying to be nice to me. This facade will go on for a while; such a person cannot change for the better. This is the worst thing that Papa has done. He got these leaches back into our lives. As per his will, they are to be taken care of.

In his words, he had written,

"Abby, I know you would never understand this being a single child. I know they don't deserve anything, least my kindness, but I can't abandon them. You will not like it.

Their sins cannot be forgiven but can be forgotten. You would be all alone after me, and even though they are not virtuous people, I want you to be surrounded by your relatives.

With time, you and they will learn to trust and support each other."

I am unsure if I could ever grow that much care in my heart to forgive or forget their actions, but I respect my father's wishes and tolerate them.

Hinal seems to be interested in Shay. He, too, is reciprocating. I am delighted for them.

Ihit seems to be settling comfortably in the office.

In short, everything is getting fast toward a fairer future, but still, something is amiss. There is emptiness and unnamed sorrow in my heart.

Even Abeer appears to be distant.

Abby.

Hinal was Shay's previous girlfriend, whom Abby referred to in her fight with Shay, that the public prosecutor had brought in repeatedly during the court hearings.

31st December

Dear C,

Innumerable things changed the course of my life this year.

I was tucked in bed by Papa and woke up to a unaccustomed

world without him. I lived in my own world, was it vanished into thin air.

The world I lived in was nonexistent, and the world I found myself in was not what I wanted.

I was helpless, in a maze with no path out. That was the year for me.

Towards the end of the year, somehow, I got a grip on myself. Even with tight business schedules, I manage to steal some time for my dance. It helps me to be me.

Abby.

A Friend

4 years ago || Abby's age – 19 years

Ihit picked up another diary. This is the phase of Abby's life that he partially shared. Still, it was unalike knowing Abby like this. It felt as if she was talking to him, a heart-to-heart talk.

2nd February

Dear C,

The year has started on a promising note. Cena Cosmica has made a profit; we are in expansion mode. I am working on plans.

Today, sent feelers to a German group. I knew they were visiting India for a destination wedding. I invited them over for a cocktail. They seemed to be interested. We may get into a joint venture on German soil.

I am dead tired but so ecstatic that I can't contain it. Definitely, I will turn Papa's dream into a reality.

I am confident Papa is watching me now. Is he happy? My hard work is just beginning to harvest fruit.

Bless me, Papa and Mom,

Abby.

25th April

Dearest C,

Today, I found a friend in Ihit. Since the day he came over, he has worked hard. Our initial meetings were strictly professional. But, gradually, we came to know each other. He is charming and has something in him that makes him so remarkable. I mean, one can undoubtedly trust him. He is a excellent listener. He listens to every problem acutely and evaluates every word before speaking. He seems to have a solution for every situation.

It's strange, from a simple staff he has become a reliable friend. The best thing that I like about him is that he respects everybody.

I am fortunate to find a friend like Ihit.

Abby

7th May

Dear C,

I need help understanding what happened? Shay and Hinal have broken up. It was sudden and brutal for Hinal.

I can't even describe the state in which Hinal is. I went to her place just like that and what I saw was shocking! Shay's photographs were all over the place. She kept clutching Shay's pictures one after another, repeating, 'Shay, you can't leave me. You can't go away.'

She was delirious.

From her blabbering, I could figure that Shay called her up in the morning to tell her it was over.

I am in a fix. Should I speak to Shay now? Or let them sort it out themselves. These things are expected in any relationship. I hope they are back together soon.

Hinal is a loved friend. I don't want to lose her.

Wishing on a dying comet - Abby.

Ihit knew about Hinal. Even Shay had confessed that he had practically ruined Hinal's life. That was why he did not bring up Shay's character or emotional stability during the court hearings. So instead of proving Shay's innocence, Ihit scrupulously steered the whole case to question the death of Abby as suicide. Abby's words proved how right he was.

14th June

Dear C,

More than a month has passed since their breakup, but Hinal's condition has worsened instead of recovering. Shay has broken all communication with her, blocked her number, and does not meet her. Hinal is on the verge of a mental breakdown; she is unstable, and her career is gone.

I tried to speak to Shay, but he avoided the topic, making it clear that it was none of my business. So I will never talk to Shay about this.

I said everything to Ihit. Though he, like me, cannot do anything, he listened. Felt a lot better talking to him.

Ihit has invited me for dinner tomorrow. I accepted it without any clue about the venue. He said he was working on it and would pick me up. I am curious.

Abby.

Ihit remembered that dinner. Memories of that dinner brought a smile to his face. Ihit's initial plan was to cook for her, but then the preparation in the morning turned out poorly. He dropped the idea. When he went to pick up Abby end of the day, she was dead tired. He was expecting Abby to cancel the dinner. She did not.

She smiled and asked, "Ihit, would you mind if I go to Cena Cosmica first? Have some work there. It would take 15 minutes. And we can go for dinner."

"Yes, of course."

"By the way, where are we going?"

"No, I thought I would cook for you. Turns out it wasn't a bright idea."

"Well, you have all the time in the world till we reach Cena Cosmica to pick a venue."

Abby was in a simple black dress. She was so tired that she could not keep her eyes open. She dozed off on her way to the restaurant.

Ihit knew it was impolite and dangerous to keep looking at the passenger seat beside him, but he could not help it. She looked so beautiful. Mercifully, the restaurant was just a short distance away. She woke up when a car came to a halt.

Next time, Ihit thought he would pick her up on a bike. That ride would never be possible now. Ihit turned a page.

15th June

Dear C,

It was such a hectic day. I almost called up Ihit to cancel the dinner. But I am so glad I didn't.

Meeting after meeting, I had no time to grab a bite. All I wanted was to turn in early. I thought of calling Ihit, but something typically came up. I forgot until the receptionist called to inform me that Ihit was in the lobby. I could not cancel.

Thankfully, I did go out for dinner. It was a much-needed break. Although I cannot recall what we spoke about, I smiled, laughed, and enjoyed it.

Night night,

Abby

15th August

Dear C,

Happy Independence Day.

I was back in school. This time, I was invited as a chief guest to my school. Yet, the school is still the same, the unchanged madness, the laughter in the corridors, and the intimidating silence during tests. The walls resonate with memories of days gone by.

It made me feel how much I lost this year. I look back at those children with a tint of envy that maturity has for the age of innocence and hope.

Remembering old me, Abby.

4th November

Dear C,

Today would make it to my list of the top 10 most irritating days of my life. Nothing went right.

First, we could not crack the deal I was aiming at.

Second, Ihit and I had a bitter difference of opinion on a particular issue. As the argument continued, we stopped discussing the case and started debating each other's approach. We were finding faults in each other. Since when did we become so close? Such traits are reserved for close friends, Ihit, and I are not that close friends. Or are we, and we just do not know it.

Thinking about it now, I should not have lost my cool. Ihit was partially correct. Still, he should not have spoken to me the way he did. He should have at least said sorry. Wait, a call. Well!!! From Ihit! Please wait for me, C. I will come back to you after the call and update you.

He called up to say sorry. I, too, told him sorry. We are friends again. So what we fought, it is okay. Differences are integral to any relationship, be it professional or friendship. The important thing is how we resolve it and still be what we are.

Abby.

31st December

Dear C,

Another year has ended, and we are already into a new one. And I have just returned home. It is already 3:00 am, and I am tired. I will be brief.

This year, I have laid a strong foundation for future.

About mistakes, I did commit one which was not less than a crime. I introduced Hinal to Shay. I feel partly responsible for the mental trauma Hinal went through.

Abby

Some diaries were still left unread. Even time was moving nonchalantly in tips and toes not to wake up the ghost of the past by the crisp rustle of pages of diaries. However, memories did stir.

Memories, they seldom sit silently. Instead, the sob of the memories' echo in the heart. Ihit was going through such a time when his memories were speaking to him through Abby's handwriting. Ihit picked up the following year's diary.

16th March

Dear C,

I love 'Abeer' so much.

Ihit took a deep breath, almost closing the diary. These were bare thoughts of a 19-year-old. He felt he was invading her privacy. He kept down the journal and walked to the window.

The dusk was settling soon, and the crimson in the sky was disappearing fast. The temperature was dropping. Ihit shivered, hair at the back of his neck standing up. He could feel AV smiling at him. Her eyes seemed to follow him; her smile was engraved in his eyes. His eyes were tired, and he wanted nothing more than to sleep off. But then there was his close friend, Abby, ready to share her life with him. He went back to the diaries.

Abeer, I have not seen him, neither have I heard him. I wonder if he exists. Yet, somewhere deep inside, I know he is there. The man who is created for me. He is there for me. Someday, somehow, I would meet him.

I have not seen him, not even in my dreams. Yet, I know one day, we will meet. Then, he would know how I feel about him.

We have a strong connection. Whenever I am in distress or

unhappy, I feel Abeer around me. Isn't that feeling great! I could almost hear his husky voice saying, 'You are my Abby. You can't sit like this. Come on, you are a fighter. I am with you. Come on, Abby. I know you can do it.' I know he is there for me. But does he feel my presence the way I do?

Abby.

28th April

Dearest C,

Today, I went to a painting exhibition. A lifetime ago, I enjoyed painting. But I never got to learn it. As a result, the dream of creating masterpieces on canvas is long gone. Truth be told, I was not that good, just average or below it. So these days, I just enjoy seeing them.

In the exhibition, I met Mahira. She is a lovely person. Somehow, she reminds me of Hinal. It has been some time since I met her. I hope she is better.

Mahira is an outstanding artist; her colors have a touch of sensitivity and hope. In addition, I found her to be down-to-earth. Naturally, I enjoy the company of such people.

Abby

3rd May

Dear C,

Everything is working nicely. There is constant and steep growth. As of today, the Cena Cosmica group is at the top. It was not easy; it took the hard work of my entire staff and me. Special mention of Ihit here. He has become more than just an advocate.

He is like a friend; he does give useful suggestions. I am lucky that he joined my group.

These successes seem like tiny steps when I think about what I must achieve. "I have miles to go before I sleep." I am unclear how.... I would somehow be successful. It may take time, but it will happen.

Abby.

Cena Cosmica was AV's passion. Cena Cosmica has always been a theme restaurant. But after AV took over, she changed it. The painted walls and ceiling with the planetary system and astronauts; things were altered. She invited him for dinner within the first month of his joining the group. Ihit was awestruck at the experience.

Ihit felt he had stepped into space as he walked through the air-lock door that was opened by the staff dressed as an astronaut. The ground felt different. It seemed buoyant as if the gravity had unexpectedly decreased. The astronaut switched the arm torch on the wrist to guide him as his eyes adjusted to the light.

"Ihit, AV has asked me to give you a tour of the restaurant. She would be joining you shortly." The name on the badge was Ensign Roop.

In a massive room, circular tables and chairs were all white and looked like steel. The ceiling was projected with a 3-D view of a person flying in the galaxy from one planet to another. The circular dome made the projection look to encompass the world.

"This is our Mess Hall," the guide explained. "This is for those brave hearts and explorers who go on voyages in starships across galaxies. So welcome; together, we explore the hidden realms."

"Is your boss a Trekkie?" Ihit chuckled.

"Is that not so obvious?"

"Of course, however you twist them, those lines remain the same."

Ihit was more of a Star Wars fan than Star Trek.

"You know we have a Bridge too. That section is exclusive for events. Here the chief guests are the ones who are in the senior officers' posts. It can accommodate 150 guests, I mean crew." They shared a laugh.

As they walked past the hall, the room temperature dipped, and there was dust like snow falling on his dark jacket. Ihit looked up. They were on a frozen planet with a blizzard about to hit them. Appreciatively, not as intense as on the planet's surface. Nevertheless, the Mess Hall had become a colder and breezy.

"Are you okay with the heights?"

"We can go to a section for daredevils. This is called the skywalk." The lift halted on the first floor, and they stepped into what looked like the void. They were on an elevated landing of around 5 feet. Glass-walk circular path around the lift linking them to the glass platforms with a table for 4-8. It could accommodate 20-30 people, and now there were none. Ensign switched on the remote, and the glass beneath them came alive. They were in a nebula. Although they could feel the ground beneath them, it still felt like they were standing in a void. They could feel the cold mist on them as the red, blue, and violet clouds of diffused dust whirled around them. They passed that section to the final one, the most sought-after area. The private quarters! The space was covered with white domes of varied sizes, from 2 seaters to four-seaters. Most of them were two-seaters. Ensign opened the door and asked Ihit to take a seat. AV would be joining him. Before she left, she asked him to choose his preference for the ambiance.

A voice filled the dome.

"Welcome," a computerized voice greeted. "Please pick up the destination for the space flight."

An exciting tour of a nebula, Mars on wheels, Flight to Venus, Andromeda Galaxy tour, Water World of Athena, Romantic getaway on Risa, Sector 57 of Feranginaar, and so on …

On an impulse, he clicked Risa. The dome changed. There was warmth around, the sky was of shades of pink, blue, and orange bordering the water bodies, and the echoes of waves breaking on the rocks filled the air. A spray of mist fell on Ihit at irregular intervals.

AV joined in a while.

"I am starving, Ihit. Let us order first and then talk shop." AV said, ignoring the ambiance around.

"It's beautiful, but let me figure out what to order. The names are alien."

Abby laughed; it filled the dome-like clinking glasses of champagne.

"The names are fancy, based on diverse worlds, but don't you worry, they have a description given below each name. I would help you."

"One question, AV. How much did this antigravity cost you?" Ihit asked.

Abby smiled with pride, "Much lesser than you expect. And it is not antigravity. Its Indian frugal innovation! The underneath of carpeting is a thin layer of air bubbles. That gives the floor a bounce.

Pages fluttered. Ihit turned his attention back to the diary.

30th June

Dearest C,

I was just asleep for moments. Then, in my dreams, I heard Abeer's voice again. It was such a beautiful feeling. I saw that I was sitting alone in my school's church. I was of my present age, and it was night. I sat there for a long time. I had something weight on my mind. I had no idea what it was.

Candles, hundreds of them, were burning all around. The entire church was lit up by the light of these candles and diffused light of the moon filtering down from the painted glass. Tears were brimming in my eyes. I was sad. Looking up through the tears, I said, 'why don't I see you?'

I felt him close to me. It seemed as if he was standing behind me. He leaned a bit over my shoulder to whisper, 'I am so close to you that you can't see me.' Then I woke up. Dawn was just breaking. People say dreams of this time come with the power of prediction. If so, Abeer is prodigiously close to me.

Abby.

In Love

3 years ago || Abby's age – 20 years

Ihit got up; his eyes were red from reading and reminiscing. He walked up to his bar and poured himself a drink. Looking at the life of a close friend through her own words when she is no more was painful.

9th August

Dear C,

Of late, I am feeling the presence of Abeer a lot more frequently than earlier. Is Abeer close to me, and my soul has recognized him, though I am blissfully unaware?

Today, we passed a decision to spend 5% of the profit from our restaurants on the welfare of HIV-positive children.

A month back, I had been to Asha, a special home for these children. They were so cheerful. They had no idea that death was constantly following them.

For these innocent kids, a cruel thing like death is nothing but an angel. For them, death is nothing more than a process for them to become a star in the heavens. But do we become stars, or do we just fade away? Is death a respite?

Ihit looked up like his gaze was penetrating through the ceiling. He was trying to see the stars. Was Abby shining as one of them? Reading the page, he could feel her strange fascination for death.

Was it a premonition? Did she know that death would be coming for her so soon? He could not read anymore. He turned a few pages.

25th September

Dear C,

Today, Ihit called me up if he could see me after office. I was in no mood for any business talk. I asked him, 'Ihit wants to meet me or advocate Ihit is asking for an appointment?'

'It is not advocate Ihit. It is just Ihit.'

'Who Ihit, my friend Ihit or just Ihit?'

'My friends are envious of me because I am counted as one of the limited friends Ms. AV has.'

'Okay, friend Ihit can drop in and surprise me.'

'Then I'll just drop in.'

Can you beat it; he came just after 30 minutes with a gift. He said it was a surprise. Can you imagine what was there? After opening seven boxes wrapped in seven layers of gift papers, I found a collection of western music.

When I said I wanted to gift him something, he gave me just 15 seconds to think. So his gift would be anything that came to my mind in 15 seconds.

What flashed in my mind was you, my beloved friend, diary. Therefore, after I am no more, I can entrust you to another treasured friend, Ihit.

I would make such arrangements that you are sent to him and all of your previous and future avatars after my death.

At times, I feel so blessed. I have Abeer to love me and his faith in me to pull me through the rough phases. I also have a friend in Ihit. Abeer keeps my heart beating, romantic and dreamy, and Ihit keeps me real.

Abby.

18th October

Dear C,

It was the most disturbing birthday I had. At my party, I invited Mahira. The way Shay looked at her was disconcerting. He is interested in Mahira the equivalent way he was with Hinal. Will history be repeated?

I will do something to stop these things from going out of hand. I hope Mahira is not foolhardy to love Shay.

Abby.

31st December

Dear C,

We made a great deal of development in our restaurants. We have tied up with the leading OTA in the country. We have also reduced carbon footprinting.

Looking forward to the coming year, Abby.

The evening had turned into night. Ihit had been reading the diaries since lunchtime. Ihit came home right away after the judgment in the morning. He had kept his calendar free for the entire day.

He got up and poured himself another stiff drink. He had not grieved for his friend, Abby. He knew he would do it once he saved the accused, Shay. He felt the time to tell Abby goodbye was after resolving the court case of her death.

Today was his day to grieve and perhaps to bid Abby goodbye. He picked up another diary of Abby.

12th January

Dear C,

Ihit had something important to share. He remained silent. At end, he said I must wait. Weird! Anyway, his surprise was terrific.

I am looking forward to it.

Abby.

14th February

Dear C,

Ihit proposed to me! …..

Ihit did not require to read it any further. Ihit could accurately recall that evening of 14th February when he had invited her for dinner. How could he forget it? Memories mirrored in his eyes. He closed his eyes to swim back in the stream of time.

Ihit had never mixed his personal life with his professional life. He had always maintained a distance between his clients. He never let anybody get any closer to him. There was always an ice wall around him. Though nobody could label him unfriendly, he was not eager to make friends. The ones who knocked at the door of his heart, gained access, and those were limited. Less than the ones counted in one hand.

Abby, too was like him. He saw his reflection in Abby and Abby's reflection in him. That was why he knew that unaffected by anything, demeanor was nothing but a mask. Beneath that cold, uncaring garb was a warm, trusting, caring, sensitive, fun-loving person that no one knew.

Ihit knew that Abby was not as joyful as she wanted others to believe. She had lost her father and had to jump in to take care of the business when she was just an adult. Yet she took it up effectively.

Time did not heal Abby's wounds, as Ihit had hoped. She had turned into almost a workaholic, certainly eroding herself. She could not confide in her friends to help her cope with her grief. Something moved in his heart. He had no control over it. He found himself trying to interact with her often on a personal level. He was not too happy with this change, but something made him do it. He could not help it.

Winning Abby's trust as a friend was exceedingly difficult. She was either noticeably introvert or had become so after her father's death. She had locked herself in some closet, and if somebody came closer to the closet, she would add more locks.

Ihit had to first unlock himself; breaking his ice wall for her. He took minor steps to become friendly. He talked about himself, his likes, and dislikes. Gradually Abby opened up. She started with her dislikes, and Ihit listened. There were uncanny similarities between her and Ihit. They enjoyed common likes and dislikes but never tried to argue over differences. They respected it.

When Ihit won her trust, Abby started sharing as much as her inner child allowed her. Abby was an indefinite layer of the puzzle. Every time he understood and solved one mystery, it would lead to another. The veils around her had utterly hidden her, and he was unwrapping one layer after another.

They became a fast friend. They shared fortunate and awful moments together. With time the bond grew stronger. In Ihit's mind, as a human being, Abby got more important than Abby the friend. Ihit found himself being dragged into her thoughts.

They were just friends but still the way she respected him had won him over. She proved a respectful listener than him. Somehow, she had an uncanny ability to sense when he was upset and would somehow make him talk. He always felt chirpier after meeting or talking to her.

A Proposal

2 years ago Abby's age – 21 years

Ihit needed another stiff drink to relive those days again.

He could just stop reading those silly diaries.

Why am I reading them? Why am I reliving those bygone days?

When had I ever refused her when she wanted to talk to me?

Abby wants to confide in me once again. She is talking to me again through the diaries' pages, and I crave to listen to her for once.

He went back to the past.

Abby, as a friend, was getting blurred in her place was Abby with whom he could see his future. He wanted her in his life for eternity.

This feeling had crept in stages, steadily. It took about one and a half years for Ihit to realize that he wants Abby more as a life partner than a friend. Sadly, Abby could not see the changes in Ihit. He was still an excellent and close friend. So it was a big surprise for her when he proposed to her. She was taken aback.

At first, Abby thought it was a prank, but when she saw his eyes, she realized the truth. She realized whatever

Ihit said was true. Abby was confused. Deliberately picking up the words, she replied, "Ihit, you are a nice person. All along, I took you as a close friend. I never thought you would propose to me. I was not prepared for it."

"Abby, what are you saying?"

"Nothing. What can I say, Ihit? I can't think."

"Think. I am waiting for your reply."

"It is not as simple. It is the decision of my life that I do not take so lightly. My life would change forever with whatever I decide. Ihit, I hope you understand; I need time."

"How much time, 1 day, 1 month …."

"I can't give you any time frame. Please trust me on this. Whenever I decide, you will be the first person to know. If you find somebody else before I tell you, it is fine with me. Do not wait for me."

"Okay, I will wait."

"One more thing, I promise I would think, but until I have replied to you, please do not remind me or ask me to hurry up. Be assured that I will not forget whatever you have told me."

"Count me on that. Another thing Abby whatever you decide, I would respect it. I am and will always be your friend. But I want our friendship to graduate to love and not be demoted to strangers. I would never …."

"It will never happen. I would never let you go. You are my friend and will always be one no matter what."

"I have unerring faith you will come to me, Abby. Love has immense power to turn fantasy into reality."

That was the first time Ihit spoke of his feeling for Abby. She needed time that he understood and respected. He never reminded her.

Abby's diary in Ihit's hand wanted attention. He continued reading.

It is not correct. How can Ihit try to be Abeer? Not that anybody knows about Abeer except me. Ihit is a nice person, but he is not Abeer. Ihit is my friend, and Abeer is my love. The distinction is clear, with a hell of a difference between the two. I don't know how long Ihit has been in love with me. Its indisputable there is some misunderstanding somewhere. He can't be in love with me. I would have seen it.

I am already in love. In mad love with Abeer. So how can I love Ihit?

I am confused as to why this has happened. I did not expect such a thing from Ihit. He wants to be Abeer. Can he be my Abeer? No, even the thought seems ridiculous.

Ihit is gentle and sober. His presence fills the space around me. He is a person who has attained dizzying heights through his own effort. He is reasonable. He never pushes his point of view on anybody. He is logical. He does not argue. All he does is explain, convince, and sometimes get convinced. He is realistic and never gets driven by passion. Does he have something called passion in him? He is a perfect perfectionist. I don't want an ideal person in my life. It's boring and dull. A person must have something that gives him a darker shade or two. It wouldn't be exciting to lead a life with someone so sensible without a wild part in him. I can respect such people, but love for me is associated with passion.

Abeer is entirely different.

Abeer has a fire in him. Whenever he is near me, till now, which is purely in my dreams or dream-like state, I am on fire too. The more this fire burns me, the finer I feel. He is so passionate and impulsive. He loves to argue about anything, and everything he thinks is right. His emotions could be his undoing. But, in the end, his heart drives him, not his mind. Faults like this make me love him even more.

I respect Ihit but love Abeer.

Abby

6th April

Dear C,

It is Ihit's birthday today. Since he has never celebrated it, I am planning it for him this year. I invited him to spend the evening together. We spent a lovely evening together, though every minute I apprehended he would start something I was unprepared for. I am so grateful that he was silent about his love for me. Would it be is or was? Has he forgotten that I had to answer him? Does not seem so. At times, I see that wait in his eyes. I am still deciding. The best part is we are still the same. Valentine's day is not between us anymore.

Abby.

1st August

Dear C,

It has been more than 6 months I have kept Ihit waiting for my reply. He is such a gem of a person that he has not yet reminded me. Would Abeer have done the same? Yes perhaps! Or No. He would have pestered me. No, he would have banged his head on the wall to ease his anxiety as an alternative to trouble me again with the question. In this respect, both Abeer and Ihit are similar, but except for this, I don't see any similarities.

Okay, Mr. Abeer, I will give you a final chance. You have to reveal yourself before my birthday this year. If you are there for me, you will show yourself. You will come to me if you care for me, else I shall forget you like you never ever existed. So I say yes to Ihit if you do not come to me.

Tick-Tock Abeer,

Abby

18th October

Dearest C,

I was sitting in my school church. Loads of problems were troubling me. Abeer seemed to have forgotten me. He was nothing more than my imagination stretched too far.

In the group, I was progressing, but I was still too far from the set target. If I fail my Papa's final wish, I will crumble. Surrounded by these thoughts, I sat there for how long. Time passed, and evening gave way to night. Something moved in my heart. I had not cried for years. The previous time tears were in my eyes was when I took over the business. I cried today. I had no control over them. After years of dormancy, they broke loose.

I sat there crying, losing all trace of time. Then I heard footsteps. The footsteps stopped behind me. I felt the person lean towards me. His warm breath was on my neck and shoulder. I seemed familiar lot familiar. He whispered, 'You can't sit like this. You are a fighter. Come on, get up ....'

What was it – Déjà vu?

I could hear no more. These were the words of my Abeer. Surprised, I turned. I had found my Abeer. I knew he was there for me. After so many years, Abeer, you came to me as my birthday gift from God. The whole world has shrunk and become a feather of dreams floating in my eyes.

At last, Abeer, I found you.

Abby.

22nd September

Dear C,

I met Abeer again today. We usually meet. After all, I found him after so many years, and I would not let him go at any cost. I have not yet given him any hint of my feeling for him. Why hurry? Did he not take ages just to show me his face? I will make him wait for months, if not for years!

Abby.

5th November

Dear C,

I am going to Australia to meet Mr. Jeet Saxena. He was Papa's friend. I'll give details about him later but now I am thinking of something.

I am thinking about Ihit. I had kept a gift for him in his car. He said he would miss me while I was gone to Australia. I am convinced he will not miss me much after seeing my gift. He would like it even though he would not understand it fully.

As for me, this trip is necessary for my aim and equally crucial for my life. First, have to confirm my feeling for Abeer. Second, experience the intensity of my love for Abeer and know the extent of his love for me.

Hope we both come out with flying colors,

Abby

31st December

Dearest C,

The year was with so many ups to lift my spirits and so many lows to crush it throughly. I can't pen them all. The highlights are: I found my Abeer and am heading towards my goal. It looks things will go in the right direction.

Abby.

Part – III: Their Versions Of Truth

Proclivity

Two of the diaries were unread. One was Abby's latest diary, the previous year's, and the another was a journal with a black leather jacket and the name 'Abeer' written in gold. It was custom ordered. Ihit sat watching both the diaries together lie side by side. He would save Abby's for the concluding thing to read. He picked up the journal name Abeer. The first entry was:

"When I close my eyes, I feel Abby around me. We were together for four hours before her flight. She was looking forward to this visit. She is expected back in April, but yes, her visit could extend until mid of May. Will she miss me? I know, I would miss her just a mite.

Abeer."

There were no dates in the journal. Entries were separated by the signature of Abeer.

"Two days have passed, and she does not even care to call me. Does she not know that someone here is frantically waiting for her call? Why is her cell switched off? I find it difficult to believe that she is not caring towards me.

Why should I care for someone who does not care for me? I, too, do not care for her. I am just concerned. The previous time we spoke, she was in the country. Now, she is on another continent, so far off.

Is she in some problem? Call up Abby, I said call me up!!!

Abeer."

"It was around 1 am. I was too restless to sleep. I have been playing squash for about 1 and half hours. I did not even notice the phone with loud music going on.

I noticed the ring in the drop space between the music tracks. Panting and drenched in sweat, I rushed to answer the call; hoping to hear Abby's voice.

Since she has left, a strange restlessness has had its grip on me. I drown myself in work, and still, I can't sleep. I spend the rest of the time playing. It is the unchanged story tonight. I wanted to continue playing till I knocked myself out. Then I heard her voice. Everything changed.

We talked for a short time. Abby told me her work was going well and enjoyed it there. I thought she would say, 'I miss you, Honey'. She never did.

Abby would never confess. I know she missed me. Why else would she call me without any work. But Abby will never admit that she loves me. Maybe, she is deriving a special kind of fun by tormenting me with her silence. My love is stubborn; if Abby had decided to trouble me, there would be no stopping her. She may be cruel, but she is the one I love. She is my magic potion. See, all my restlessness is gone. I will shower, sleep peacefully, and dream of the day when she opens her heart and runs into my arms.

Abeer"

"Winter evening! I am writing not in the captivity of my room but on the terrace. There is unbound freedom all around. The sky is infinite blue with sprinkled gold, purple and crimson without any restriction of form or pattern. The wind that is blowing has an element of confusion.

Does my sense play tricks on me? I know Abby is not near me, yet I can see her everywhere. There, on the horizon, smiling. She is dressed in black mystery. I try reaching her, and she eludes. She adds another layer of mystery whenever I know what is in her heart and mind.

This evening, instead of uncovering veils between us, has added some.

She stands there with eyes closed, one hand behind her hair and another stretched towards the sky. A dusky-color veil came floating and draped her. One after another, they kept draping her till she was merged with the heaviness surrounding me.

Can't she, for once, tear all the veils and come running to my arms.

Waiting for her always,

Abeer."

Obsession

I hit flipped some more pages. The journal entries were from one person, Abeer. He began reading randomly now.

"I abruptly remember the drive we had. It was a Sunday. I went to her place. I knew her workload on Sundays is usually lesser. We always enjoyed our Sundays. I wanted to take her to the closest forest and camp there for the night.

We left with the first ray of light for 2 hours. She was so cheerful and carefree. We camped. We made our makeshift stove with branches. For people like us who live in a concrete jungle and cook over gas or microwave, this was a refreshing experience. We looked fascinated as the flavescent leaves, and twigs we collected were leisurely getting consumed by hungry fire. Smoke rose as unhurriedly fingers of fire touched each leaf.

Abby was a uneasy with the smoke. There were tears in her eyes with smoke and onions that she was chopping. Yet, Abby was still enjoying the experience. She had hairs out of her band, tears, cough, and a smidgen ash stain on her left cheek, yet she looked stunning.

We enjoyed the best time together. We cooked, explored a measure of the jungle, and thought of leaving the camp towards the evening. But, the jeep would not start. In a dense jungle, evening falls much before the rest of the world. And in such a world, you would not expect a mobile signal. So we started our long walk towards the highway.

At last, we found the highway where we found some help. It was after hours of repair we hit the road. I am somewhere glad that we did not find help sooner.

It was late and a day hard walk that tired her out. I could see her trying in vain to keep her eyes open. Inexorably, she slipped into a deep sleep.

I will never forget that ride. Abby was sleeping with her head on the windowpane. Occasionally her hair would fall on her face, and she would knit her brows; and a smile on her lips. Dim lights inside the jeep and occasional light on the highway made her look more beautiful. Then I realized why that sleeping princess was called 'Sleeping Beauty'.

I wish I would and could just kiss her, and she would get up from her deep spell. But, once we entered the city, the magic broke. She was again AV, not my sleeping beauty.

Oh Shit! I remember every detail of it. Grievously, as much as I would love to dream about her, I have work to do. I can't sit here all night.

Bye, Abeer."

"I am Abeer. Everything is the same, but still, nothing is the same. Something is amiss. I get up at late unlike my usual routine. I feel frightened to do so. Memories of the future, present, and past frighten me. All my confidence is waning.

Mornings are no longer cheerful, bright and sunny. Instead, they are uncommonly cold, damp, and gloomy. I get up, but then the surroundings force me back to bed. I close my eyes, not wanting to feel that heaviness invading me. But it has somehow.

My work no longer interests me like it did. Not that I am losing grip over it. I don't feel like doing anything. It is senseless confusion, I know, but I cannot help feeling void.

I am falling freely, a free fall but not under the influence of gravity to pull me. I am there, falling unreservedly into the void. Will my life also be unchanged? Waiting and waiting for Abby's reply. My life hangs in the emptiness. It is perhaps driving me crazy.

Abeer"

"Today evening brought a unusual me to me. I, Abeer of Abhiskhita, my Abby. I felt a humid hot draft sweep past my inner existence. Today I became aware of the man inside me who is obsessed with Abby. He desperately wants to hold her, feel her presence, and desire her. I may have denied his presence for a long time. But he seems too determined to get her love.

It all happened after I returned from the office and turned on the music system with Abby's favorite music collection I had borrowed. It had a long, slow dance number on the saxophone with a soft jazz beat. The music beat and warm water of my Jacuzzi were evoking my senses.

For the first time, I did not dry myself after the bath. Instead, I sat on my low couch, listening to music not through my ears but through each pore of my body. I could feel the tremor of my senses through the droplet of restless water, shivering with each beat of the music.

I closed my eyes and left my mind to drift in any direction. I wanted to surrender my days, evenings, and nights to the person in me who was languidly taking control of me. Not surprisingly, I found Abby's thoughts embedding deeper and deeper in me, in the depths of the saxophone's ecstatic number.

With my closed eyes, I saw some scintillating droplets dancing to the tune of music, leaving a stretch of sparkle through the way. Gradually those shiny dust came nearer, and then they became diamonds on somebody. I had a better look with my eyes closed. The diamonds were on Abby. Was her attire made of diamonds, or were those on her skin? She was dancing. I felt the music in my body.

I saw her face only. The rest of her was covered with tiny diamonds. Fireballs of unequal size and shape weaved the illusion of depth, dizziness, and darkness while burning her gently and steadily. They looked like they were loosely tied together, ready to fall, when she whirled around with the music flow. Each diamond shimmered as she danced, unseen, in her own world. I heard a beat. Music had occasional jazz, but that beat was not a part of the music. It was something else, something inside me. It was my heart. It was becoming more audible and was becoming faster.

At the note change of saxophone when the jazz rumbled a bit harder – whoosh – she did a swift turn on her left toe, with her right leg stretched out, left hand on her heart, and right stretched above her head. Some diamonds broke loose. I could see some portion of Abby's neck as perfected by God. I could not take my eyes away; she was blissfully unaware. The music picked up its pitch and went on to become more intense. So was Abby. She had forgotten herself and swam through the air as a nymph in heaven of desire. I felt a bitter sweetness surrounding me with an aroma of musk that aroused some unknown ancient passion inside my throbbing heart. I was just not in control of myself and found an appetizing and satiating feeling enveloping me.

Abby's movement gained momentum, and diamonds fell more mercilessly. With each step she took, she climbed higher on the rungs of ecstasy and, with ragging velocity, broke free one or two diamonds every second. I was feeling different. I had never felt like this before, and I liked it. I was exploring unexplored dimension where Abby and Abeer found themselves closer.

The floor was carpeted by diamonds. She was imperceptible; she was moving faster than my closed eyes could capture. Yet I could see the tiny images of my Abby trapped by each diamond that fell from her body and lay at her feet.

Music was on its end note. My heart was giving it a synchronized beat. I tried to follow her moves, but she was a blur. I could get a faint outline of her movement. Her thousand miniature images trapped in diamonds were being scattered by the gestures of her legs.

In the end, with the close of the crescendo of the jazz beats, she stopped. And all the diamonds broke loose from her body. Then, in the next instant, she vanished.

I opened my eyes when the music ended. I was tired and sweating profusely. The feeling was nicely lascivious, but nevertheless sacred.

Abeer."

"She plays with me. Can't she be clear? Why she does it? Am I not human? Don't I have any feelings? Why does she take me for granted? Does she ever feel the pain and trauma I am going through?

She enjoys it. Today I could not resist hinting that she has to get back to me on something important. But, instead, she just played with words, 'Why so hurry. I need time.'

Time, how much? I would leave her and move on if she said 'No' to me. But, then again, she hasn't said 'NO.'

No more. I can't take it. Neither is this girl killing me, nor is she letting me live. My head! It is bursting. I wish it exploded tonight. At least I would get rid of this waiting. Abeer."

Anger

"I did it! Something came over me, and I did it. I was getting ready for the office. I felt her watching me. Abby liked this shirt and always complimented me whenever I wore it.

I removed it and, on impulse, tore it to pieces. I was angry. I got my lighter and burnt it to ashes. I could have thrown it in my fireplace, but that would be too fast! Won't it be? I want it to burn as I do. When it was all over, I took out another shirt and went to the office.

Abeer."

"*Yesterday, I had burnt her favorite shirt, imagining I had burnt my feeling for her. If it was simple. Why did I do it? I should never have done it.*

I know what my subsequent steps are. But, first, I would go and search for an identical shirt.

When I was burning the shirt, I thought I had burnt my love for Abby. Then I saw her on fire instead of the shirt. I did not stop. I wanted to, but then somewhere, I liked seeing her burn. After all, she was experiencing what I experienced, a fire that never quenches. An eternal fire. Why do people find love such a pleasure? I have found it gives me nothing but pain and insanity.

Abeer"

"*I am so proud of her. Giving more to society than she has ever gotten from it. In Australia, she found some time to be associated with NGO that cares for old people, just like Help Age. There was another guy who headed this project, another hotelier. He had asked Abby to grace the occasion, and she stole the show.*

My eyes were just fixed on her.

Anyway, I must hurry up for the office. I am already running late.

Abeer."

"She called me! That is love, Abeer. She loves you. Why on this earth will she call you without any specific reason. I have brought an exact replica of the shirt. She will not notice the difference. Still, I said to her sorry for missing her. I just wish she would come back soon.

Abeer."

"It is already mid of May, and she has not returned. It has been a week or so she has yet to call me. Either her phone is not reachable, switched off, or is busy. I am entirely at her mercy to hear her voice. When she takes pity on me, she calls me. Why do I love this girl?

It was 2:30 am, and I was woken up by some horrible nightmare that my Abby was being snatched away by someone. Sleep has eluded me, and so I thought about writing.

Why has she not called me yet? Has she gone to some part with no connectivity? She is never this careless. She keeps her office informed, but they were also unaware of her plans this time.

Abeer"

"At last, Abby is back! Why am I on cloud nine? Assuredly, I got my life back. I wish she would come running to me and melts in my heart. I want to. I wish she tells me that her life is incomplete without me. I am dying to hold her in my arms.

Truth be told, I can never tell her. I have countless conversations with her in my mind, but when I am with her, I am different. Sometimes I feel like an imposter who has kidnapped the real me and hidden him somewhere in the dungeons.

Abeer."

Ihit flipped a few more pages.

"It was the first evening which we spent together after she came back from Australia. How stupid of me to expect a romantic evening? I took so much special care of my looks. Careless backhands shave, musk aftershave, her favorite red striped shirt, and so on. I took care of every minute detail and ordered an engagement ring with two heart-shaped diamonds.

To my distraught, it turned out to be just a casual, friendly meeting, a slightly warmer and more personal than a business review. While I was waiting every minute for Abby to speak the magic words, 'Abeer, I love you', all she talked was about Australia. Yes, she did an effective job there, but does it mean she would keep bragging about it, forgetting what I can be to her.

I still love her. Maybe she would speak these magic words later. I trust my love. I won't lose my patience.

Abeer."

"I was summoned by Ms. Workaholic to her house. She was ordered to rest by the doctor, so she brought work home instead.

What the hell she thinks she is? Will this world come to an end if she takes a day off?

Work! Work!! Work!!! Can't she think of anything else except her work? What does she work for? Workaholic! She must be taken and treated in some rehab center.

What is the use of all wealth without health? The stress and strain of continuous work have driven her to bed. She was so weak that she could not get up when I went to meet her.

Shall I confess? Even in that state, she looked beautiful. Did she call me under the pretext of work? I know the work was not urgent; it could have waited. Still, she called me, is it not love? She wanted me by her side when she was not well. This is nothing but love. It also proves that she has accepted that I am special to her. Now the wait is for her to admit that she loves me.

She looked so fragile. With half-opened dreamy pinkish eyes swelled with rheum, she appeared sensual, tender, and delicate, unlike herself. I don't want to see her in this state, sensuous or not. I just want to see her get well. I can't see her in pain.

Abeer."

"My life is not meaningless without Abby, but without her in my life, life is not worth living. I have waited long enough for my silent eloquence to speak. Sure, she understands how I feel for her, but she has not reciprocated. Maybe she needs to hear my feelings for her.

Abeer"

Ihit turned some more pages. He was about the read some more when his phone rang. Keeping a bookmark, he went and picked it up. It was 10:10pm.

"Hey, Dude, It is Shay. What happened? Why aren't you at the party?"

Ihit had utterly forgotten that Shay had thrown a party to celebrate. Although Ihit had given his consent to be there, after spending time with Abby and Abeer, he was not in the mood to. He promptly said, "Well, Shay!

Thanks, but I am sorry. I will not be able to turn up. It has been an exhausting trail. Now that it is over, I am turning in early."

Shay was disappointed, but he dropped the matter. Ihit disconnected the phone, kept it off the hook, switched off his mobile, and returned to his table. He meant to avoid further disturbances.

Both Abeer's and Abby's diaries were on the table. Abby's diary was complaining and demanding his attention. He could keep Abeer waiting but not Abby. So he picked up her journal and began reading.

Respite

7th January

Dear C,

There was one period when Papa had lost everything. At that time, Papa had a partner. A trusting person like Papa never felt the need to keep an eye on him. The partner ran away with loads of amount. We landed in significant debt. We knocked on every door for help but to no avail, including the banks. There were two options: to sell off the business to repay the loan or to sell off our control over it. Both things would have killed Papa.

Respite came in the form of Jeet Saxena.

He is a billionaire businessman and my father's friend. He brought 51% of our shares.

With this money, the debt was paid off. The problem was successfully resolved in the eleventh hour. However, Papa lost significant ownership of the group. It troubled him, and he tried to get it back. He could not; it remained a dream and was passed down to me as a responsibility. Though Mr. Saxena never interfered in the business. Nobody here knows that he is the primary partner. For everyone here, it is Papa's business.

Now that I have made a considerable amount of money, my sole aim is to become a major shareholder as soon as possible. It did not matter to Mr. Saxena as long he got his profit.

Honesty runs in our blood. Papa could have cheated his way out since Mr. Saxena was not greatly involved. After Papa, I kept on with his work. Now, I ought to buy back some shares from him. I am starting something here. It'll take some time. I should maintain our relationship and keep a chance to regain my business. Mr. Saxena is keen to hold onto high profits percentage coming from here.

Let it, I have time on my hand, and I would convince Mr. Saxena.

Abby.

20th February

Dear C,

All my efforts to convince Mr. Saxena failed. He won't budge a bit. I tried to get it without showing him how desperate I was for them. Mr. Saxena has 30% of the shares and distributed the remaining shares to his son and daughter-in-law.

Taksh Saxena has 15%, and Varsha Saxena has 6% of the stakes in the business.

That makes me the primary partner. So I have nothing to worry about for now.

Should I let it go? Still, the family combined becomes a majority shareholder by a mere 1%. Should I be worried? I don't think so. Taksh and Varsha do not see eye to eye. For security's sake, I should buy back from either of them.

Keeping my fingers crossed and my mind sharp.

Abby

15th March

Dear C,

Taksh had insisted that I spend the whole day with him. I accepted his invitation. To say the least, he was pressingly persistent. I thought it was a fun day, and I had fun plans like waves surfing, but this guy would not take no for an answer. He said there was some business to discuss that needed my input.

Taksh's whole life is about business. He has the most ambitious plan ever. A virtual life for two to seven days!

Abby

28th March

Dear C,

Taksh has an insane idea. He has purchased acres and acres of land in the middle of nowhere in Australia. And he dreams of making a 'Fantasy island' there. There would be a set up of different time periods and regions. A guest can pick a life to live for 2-7 days and get that life. I saw blueprints of the plan. There is a Roman settlement, arena, a Khali Dera, Mughal garden of Agra Fort, a human colony in some comet, Padmakishori's Lake Palace, Titanic, Spaceship, and some other periods that I needed help understanding. Everything was detailed in Taksh' presentation for bankers and authorities. But I was not positive it would fly with the authorities. The operating cost was high and has potential for damage claims or safety concerns, both physically and psychologically.

It focused on providing a guest with a life of the time of his choosing. The guest would pick up the time and role, and the rest would be unexpected. The non-playing actors would be inserted in the live story that would be taking place in that specific setup, and they would be leading that life; a respite from their everyday life to taste a fresh life filled with unexpected things. The guest also had to choose the difficulty level in their newfound lives and starting point of their stories or, as Taksh says, their story so far. It was an exciting idea. How many legal aspects had to be considered for something like this? The presentation went on with safety measures and all things that were off-limits and standard protocols.

However, looking at the customer sales pitch, I cannot but be amazed at the plan's brilliance. Had I been one of the audience, I would like to be in this world and taste another life for a few days.

Creating a theme restaurant cost a bomb; how would he fund this insane idea? He told me that Cena Cosmica gave him the inspiration. And his marketing agents had done some study to show that such a thing would be an instant hit. Of course, it would take money for details, without which the initiatives will be a cheap show. But, with profitable investment and customer experience, a disruptor the world is waiting for.

I am not confident of all this except that it is an ambitious project. Taksh has asked me to be associated with the project. I was tempted to say yes in exchange for his shares of Cena Cosmica, but I did not. It did not feel right. I told him that I would think about it.

Frankly speaking, I don't like him that much. Though I like his project. It would give me an opportunity to get his shares of Cena Cosmica, but I should be careful in dealing with him. He has a weird look in his eyes. It is troubling. He seems to be hiding something.

Abby

2nd April

Dear C,

I have developed a close relationship with Varsha. She would have sold me her shares, but it is impossible now. She and Taksh realized that they were not meant for each other. Still, they gave their relationship a shot, but it was futile. So they have decided to get divorced. It will happen sometime next month.

The 6% of the shares she has as Mrs. Taksh Saxena will return to Taksh or Jeet Saxena. Varsha is not a greedy woman; she is graceful and wants to end this relationship with equal grace. Varsha is not fighting for bigger alimony etc. She wants nothing from Taksh.

I wish there were any another way to get the shares.

Abby

6th April

Dear C,

It is my best friend's birthday. Pity I am not there to celebrate. I talked to him over the phone. He was too gloomy. I pleaded with him for over an hour to switch on his mood. I wanted to tell him about various things: Australia, me, and even Abeer. I know he would understand my love for Abeer. But, I cannot discuss this over the phone or over the net. I would tell him face to face.

Happy Birthday, Ihit,

Abby

A sad smile crossed Ihit's lips as he read the line; she remembered his birthday.

17th May

Dear C,

Today I am going back to India. The reason I came to this Island Continent was not an utter failure, though not successful either. I did not get my shares. But something else has begun. I have agreed to partake in Taksh' insane idea. In weeks or months, we will work out the details. But first, I have to discuss it with Ihit.

I have also decided something. I am now certain of my feelings for Abeer. I should have told him about my feeling on his birthday, no problem, I will tell him on my birthday. After all, I found him on my birthday; It is apt to confess my feeling on my birthday too.

Ihit, I hope you will understand the reason behind this.

Waiting to go back to my Abeer,

Abby.

5th June

Dear C,

It is about Shay. Wonder how lightly he treats love. I apprehended that something would start between him and Mahira. It happened when I was in Australia. Will Mahira, too meet the fate of Hinal? Hinal is out of trauma, but her pain continues. Her life, which was a bubbling stream, has reached a standstill.

I will not let it happen to Mahira. I will do everything to separate them. This time Shay has come up with a new card, true love. He says he wants to marry Mahira. Shame! He is my cousin. I must do something.

Abby.

28th July

Dear C,

Ihit is not well. I cannot imagine he is the guy who claimed that disease cannot touch him, is currently confined to bed. I hate seeing him in such a state. Worse, there is nobody to look after him.

These are challenging times. Doctors are satisfied with his development and his reaction to the meds. Still, something frightens me. What if the docs are lying again as they did in Papa's illness? I know things have changed, but some fears though irrational, grip my heart. No logic can ever calm these irrational fears.

Doctors report Ihit's condition to me twice a day; unlike in the past, I am in control. Still, sometimes years gone by come alive. The pain of losing my father kills me again. It makes me insecure. I can't lose a friend like Ihit.

I also saw a gift wrapped with my name on it when I searched for an ice bag in his home. He had no option but to let me in his sanctuary. He never invites anyone to his house. If I had not known him better, I would have thought this a trait of a serial killer. I wonder what it is and when he plans to give it to me. Maybe, I know what it is. But I am not going to talk about it.

Abby"

Ihit smiled to himself again. Leaving her diaries for him after her death showed how special he was to her. Pitifully for Ihit, too little, too late. He turned a few more pages.

Indignation

21st September

Dear C,

My love and my dreams are on opposite sides. I am expected to choose one. What can be more troublesome than choosing between my dreams and my passion? When I had planned to say everything to Abeer, this Taksh created the biggest problem of my life.

What I can't believe is his father. He was so desperate to keep the shares. He refused to sell it to me, but now he is okay to sell it in the market. I spoke to him. He said he had never seen his son so desperate for anything, and the market did not have enough trust in his project. They find it too risky to finance. 'My son's heart is fixed on that project; as a father, I wish to see him succeed.' That is precisely what the old fool, Mr. Saxena told me.

I raised funds and got some investors, but they needed convincing with Taksh's ability to pull this venture off. As much as I know Taksh is a dedicated businessman, he has an accomplished track record, and still, the market does not trust him with this project! Why?

If I find that out, I may not need to do what I think is the single option to save my Cena Cosmica.

Abby

21st September

Dear C,

I am back. The Virtual life project has an immense probability of operating in the grey areas. The venture capitalist and the top sharks do know that. It is difficult to block the people of influence from pushing the boundaries. The problem is that Taksh is an honest businessman. He has, in the past, walked away from a bunch of advantageous deals or has rubbed influential people in the wrong way. The investors feel that if these people want to indulge in something and Taksh block it, they will kill the project.

I have no option but to marry this person to get the shares designated for his wife. With these shares, I will save my Cena Cosmica.

The thing is, why would Taksh marry me and give me the shares to block his deal? I would do anything for my Cena Cosmica; equivalently, he would do anything for his project.

I have spoken to investors, and they are assured of the project if I become an active partner in his project. I would use it as a bargaining chip for the shares. "My association with his project in return for the shares I need." I will sleep over it tonight.

Abby

22nd September

Dear C,

I know what you are thinking, C dear. The single way is to convince this crazy guy that marrying me would save his pet project and my Cena Cosmica.

This time the mental turmoil is just too much. I wish that I had yet to realize who Abeer is? I was looking forward to a life with him. Now, I don't know what I would tell him. If I let Taksh have his way, I will lose Cena Cosmica, my father's dream and my sole aim in life. Cena Cosmica has always been my passion and my lifeline. And then Abeer has been my strength. I can't let any of them go.

If I marry Taksh, I will save Cena Cosmica and lose Abeer.

It pains me, but every day that option to find any alternative solution seems to diminish.

Abby

9th October

Dear C,

I asked Ihit's view on my situation.

I told him a friend was in a fix where the friend had to choose between his feelings and business. He said there are no doubts that emotions are important, but business should be prioritized. As feelings are intangible and can be relieved, business chance, once gone, will never come again.

Ihit thought the person I was talking about was Taksh.

Was his answer clouded by the fact that he never liked Taksh? Not that he said anything against him, but I have known him for a long time. Ihit does not like Taksh and prefers that we have least interactions or business with him.

If it was that easy, Ihit. That I could let my feeling go and grab the opportunity.

Abby.

18th October

Dear C,

The day I had been waiting for a long came and went without significance. Unremitting work, incessant people, unceasing parties but everything was so dead. Everything was lifeless. I wanted to say, 'Abeer, I love you', but I could not.

I wanted to confide in Ihit but could not. Will Ihit let me go and marry a person I am not in love with? Still, was it not Ihit who suggested that I should choose business over feeling?

Will Abeer understand that if I let this opportunity of getting my business back, a piece of me will die?

I am swinging from one option to another. I have never faced such a troubling question ever.

Abby.

4th November

Dear C,

As the end of this year approaches, I am getting confused and tense. My heart drags me in one direction while my mind in another. The girl in me wants to run to Abeer, to his arms, to be assured. In his arms, my life has new meaning. With Abeer, every day begins with the new Sun and ends with a promise for another.

What will life be with Taksh? It will be a compromise, the death of my wishes; which is worse than death, gradual killing, murder, strangling my desire with my own hands. I know I would die the moment Abeer walks out of my life, but the body would go on living.

Both sides of the scale have emotions. One has mine, and another has Papa. Who should get priority? Should I be selfish, ignore Papa's wish, run to Abeer or kill my desires forever.

I am still confused,

Abby.

13th December

Dear C,

I have decided. I have no right to enjoy my life if I have not fulfilled my duties well. It sounds harsh. Truth is, I would not be happy. My guilt would follow me. Power and privileges never come cheap. Papa gave this life to me, in return, expected me to get back the majority shares of the group.

I have put in my proposal to Taksh. He was surprised, but the businessman in him did recognize the win-win scenario. I get my Cena Cosmica, my life, and his pet project sees the light of day. We have agreed that if everything goes as per the plan, then the day his project is inaugurated (ballpark 6-8 months from today). I would get 5% of his shares in addition to those I get by marrying him. These shares are mine, irrespective of marital status. Compared to his pet project Cena Cosmica means nothing. The project that was stuck has gotten alive once again. Somewhere, Taksh realizes that it is due to my association with his pet project! He is a bit grateful, which is why he has agreed to transfer 5% of his shares of Cena Cosmica to me.

I am sorry, Abeer. Alas, I can't confide in you.

I wish I had told you about my feelings before all this happened.

Now, it is too late.

How would I ever tell him that I love him, but I love Cena Cosmica more? First, I will have to marry Taksh to bail us out of this precarious condition. It would take almost a year or so. After that, when I am the major shareholder, I would divorce Taksh (assuming he married me to save his pet project and has no feelings for me). Then I will return, and we will live happily ever after. (again, assuming nobody comes into Abeer's life and he is waiting for me). It sounds so ridiculous!

Wished, I had told him about my feeling and he had confessed about his too. Right now, I am curious if he loves me back or not. But we have yet to create that area of trust. I can't imagine how anybody on this earth would react if someone confided their love in this way, with so countless strings attached.

It is appropriate that I never breathe a word about this to Abeer. Let things flow, and I will take my chances after a year. There are too various moving parts, and the water is too muddy. Let this time heal me and still the water. I will wait for a time when I can tell my Abeer all that is in my heart.

Today is not that day.

Abby

15th December

Dear C,

Is it supposed to be romantic? I received a packet with a big rock that Taksh had ordered; an engagement ring from a catalog. The ring is beautiful but feels heavier. I have it on the nightstand. I will put it on once I deboard from the flight.

Anyway, I will tell Abeer that I have planned to go away. I would say to him on the 30th of the month. On the 1st of next month, I will be in Australia.

Abby.

30th December

Dear C,

When I look back, I find images or may be a mirage of my desire, myself, and Abeer. I also see Ihit, a friend with whom I have shared my achievement and bitter-sweet memories. I would miss a friend like him. I would be the major shareholder of my group, but then I would also be Mrs. Taksh Saxena, and she is not Abby.

Then there would be geographical distance and two homes. I would be flying from one home to another, taking care of the group, and then returning to Australia. I would not get time for my friends as I do now. As an active partner, I would also be taking care of Taksh' pet project. Sooner it launches, the better. I get complete control of Cena Cosmica.

Abeer, I wish I never had dreamt about him, and if I did, I hoped it never came true. My solitary relief is that I did not confess my feeling for him, and neither did he explicitly say that he loves me, but I know that he loved me all along. However, now I wish that my wishful thinking had remained a wish.

I wish I had confessed my feeling before this mess came into my life courtesy of Taksh; things would have been different. I have wronged you, Abeer. I wish you would punish me, Abeer.

I told Abeer that from the 1st, I would go away. I told him that I was to marry Taksh to get the shares. I told him about the story that Papa had confided in me about the group. I told him everything except that I loved him.

Abeer heard everything, but with no change of expression on his face. I hurt him deep inside.

There were no scars on the surface. Every word of mine sank too deep into the core of Abeer's heart. In the end, he just got up, pinned a strange smile on his face, wished me good luck for the future, and left without a second look.

I have invited him to my farmhouse tomorrow; to spend the ultimate evening of the year with him. He said nothing; I know he will not turn me down.

Abby.

31st December

Dear C,

This is the final day of the year and my life as I know it. Tomorrow's Sun will bring hope and dreams to people around the world. But, it'll land me in a place where I'll find no known face. A loveless place is a place where the heart does not throb. Life with such a man whom I neither love nor respect is not a life at all.

Life has become a compromise. I am thinking of coming clean with Abeer, yet it may be too late, for I wonder if he would still be with me. I might lose him forever.

I don't want to think about tomorrow. Tomorrow will come, and I will endure it, with or without Abeer. Today is what I have control over. Today is mine. It is EXCLUSIVELY MINE! I would spend it with Abeer.

I'll make these fast fleeting hours heaven for both of us. It will be such an evening that neither of us can forget till our deaths.

I may hope to return to Abeer, but who is to say what is in Abeer's mind. Will he move on? Will there be someone else who would replace me in his heart? I am conveniently assuming he loves me. He did not protest when I told him my plan? Am I absolutely certain that he loves me?

All I know, I love him, and this could decisively be our long and permanent separation. I must make this a memorable night for us. Memories of 31st Dec will always smell afresh in our minds.

This night changes both of our lives forever,

Abby.

Helpless

Abby's diary came to an end. Ihit collected all her diaries and kept them on his shelf. Now Abeer's diary was left on the table half read. Covering his eyes, Ihit sat thinking about Abby. Abby had so sundry of feelings and emotions, and he was unaware of them. She was a guarded person, never letting anyone peep into the deepest of her sentiments. Now Ihit knew them all. Abby was talking to him through the pages of her diary. Now Abby would never write anymore.

Ihit flipped some pages of Abeer's journal.

"My work demands a lot these days. Worst it is driving me away from Abby. Four days have passed, and I am yet to meet her. Where is my obsession leading me? Can I have a single day when my heart is not pierced by her thoughts? Pity, she is ignorant of this. Is it true that she is ignorant?

It is not her fault. Those deep dark eyes stole my heart when she set them on me. Those eyelashes have entangled me, and I find myself on a silken web that can never be broken by poor prey. This prey does not want to be freed. I may have a way with words in my circle, but writing is never my forte. I don't know if I could ever express what I feel.

Abeer."

"Eight days have passed since I returned home. I was on a business trip with some clients away from my city. Big deal! I met her but did not dare to present something I had for her; a dress.

On my way back, I saw this dress on a mannequin. I knew the dress would look lovelier on my Abby. So I brought it, but not knowing how to present it to her? This is the first time I have gifted something like this. What if she dislikes it?

It is still wrapped in glossy pink paper with her name on it. Somehow will gather some courage and present it to her. What if she rejects it? I would not take her rejection well.

Abeer."

"Today, I found another facet of Abby. A door opened, and I caught a glimpse of Abby that I never knew existed. Who was that Abby I met today?

As usual, I was on my lawn with the first smile of the Sun, exercising. I always felt nice to be out to feel the coolness of the surroundings to the day's warmth. I feel great exercising when the Sun is tender, the flowers lazily opening their eyes, and birds chirp in a slow, graceful tone. I like to see the transition from dawn to morning on my lawn working out.

It was morning already, though early by any definition; around 7:00 am. I felt a notch stranger; I turned and saw Abby. I am curious to know how long she was sitting there watching me. I felt awkward and tongue-tied. Then, she started, 'You carry on. It was Sunday; I had no work in the morning, so I dropped in early. Please continue; it's rare to watch such a well-built man exercise.'

There was an awkward silence. I was tongue-tied.

'Subject to your comfort level.' She added.

Of course, I was uncomfortable, but something in her voice urged me to continue. Sheepishly, I smiled and started my push-up. I could feel her eyes on me. At a distance, I could see her surrounded by a tornado of weird thoughts that I could not understand. Those eyes with the storm were watching me. I was shaken inside; I was restless like a quivering leaf.

Did I honestly not understand the language of her eyes, or did I know it perfectly?

Abeer"

"It's August; it is autumn. It is the time when all old leaves are shed. Mourning time, time for all detachments and heart aches. Dusty roads and paths are filled with dry leaves broken from their love, the trees creaking and squealing under the heavy footgear of the passerby.

She has yet to reply. I, too, feel broken and detached from my base, wandering aimlessly and endlessly, swept here and there by the wind to be crushed every day, every hour, minute, and seconds by my own expectation and her delay.

Ah! Why did I love such a heartless person? What is the use of crying when I have gone too far to retrace my steps? Feelings are not calculations, and that to one can correct once a mistake is found. Feelings remain sleeping until someone knocks in, and when that happens, they can never be put to sleep anymore.

Abeer."

"I think I can be hopeful.

I have malaria and am commanded by my Abby to take a rest. But, I can write a bit. She has canceled most of her meetings to care for me. I hear her on the stairs. I must stop, or else I would get an appropriate amount of scolding from her for being on my study table. How will I not love such a person?

Abeer"

"It is the end phase of the night. The night will be lured into sleep in a few hours, and the day will wake up from deep slumber. It is

4:00 am. I am a practical man. Creativity has never been my strong suit. Yet I saw the most beautiful of all the dreams. My subconscious creativity does not have anything to do with it. The inspiration of this beautiful dream could be from the light of my life, my Abby.

I could vividly remember; I was climbing a bare mountain. Soon I came upon a cave-like opening. I went inside it. After walking a distance, I found some light from an unidentified source. I walked in the direction of light.

There was ample clearance inside the rock caves. In the middle of the clearing was a mirror house; a house made up of pieces of mirrors. A single beam of light fell on it, but the mirrors reflected them all around to light up the surrounding. The view looked even more spectacular, with a modest brook falling from an edge of a rock cut just above the house. It kept on rinsing one side of the mirror house.

I walked near the door. The mirror door opened with wind chimes of glass singing. I stepped in. The whole interior was made up of glass and mirrors. I walked from one room to another until I came to an escalator made of transparent glass. My eyes were wide open with fascination and with a bit of apprehension. I was on a transparent floor. If I did not remind myself that I was on the glass, it felt like I was walking in thin air. I reached the first floor, and again, a translucent room beckoned me in.

The walls, till one-third of their height, were made up of mirror; the rest were glass, translucent, frosty glass. I felt a chill down my spine. Was I standing on some ice world? The ceiling was made up of mirrors, but the floor was made of transparent glass. The grass cultivated on the ground floor was clearly visible. It created a strange combination of closeness and distance. So near and yet so far!

In the middle of the room was a sofa made of glass; smooth and curvy. A low-height center table was also made up of shining glass. A bowl of cherries and black currant adored it, along with a mirrored 'surahi[15]' of 'Omar Khayyam.' It was so beautiful, but it was cold and lifeless.

Suddenly, life busted into the room with its full vigor. Abby, dressed in shiny black dress and glass shoes, with eyes half closed, came into the room. Chill turned in hot steam when she glided like a swan across the room to decisively curl up like a cat on the sofa. Lost in some dreams, Abby went on biting her red, nervous, quivering lower lips while one hand played with her hair. She appeared to be wholly engrossed in her own thoughts that my presence had no effect on her; not noticing me. (Does she ever see the real me!)

The octagonal room reflected her everywhere I turned. Wherever I looked, I saw her. I was rooted in my place. Then, after a while, like a sleeping serpent, she stood up sluggishly and stretched herself to full. She smiled at an unknown thought. Then sat royally on her sofa with her back resting on its head and another stretch full on the couch. She picked up cherries and tasted black currants. Then somewhere, my eyes could not catch where she fished out a cup. The cup seemed to be made of a customed single piece of diamond. The rock was as big as an ostrich's egg and was fashioned to make a cup.

The fire and purity of the diamond cup were enough to rivet my eyes, but then Abby poured bright red sherbet into the cup. Some facets of the diamond reflected sherbet pouring into the cup as it clashed against its walls. Some mirrored the surroundings; some trapped the falling light, while others emitted it. It was all chaos,

---

[15] *Surahi – Generally made of clay, glass or brass, it is a pot with long neck for storing or serving water or wine.*

confusion of light, fiery sparkle, letting loose the light and trapping it again. With all these commotions on, she lifted the cup to her lips, pressing tender, soft lips against the hard surface of the diamond cup.

Abby was sipping from the cup. With each sip she took, I became thirstier. Abby took her time tasting it to test its patience and the wait to touch her lips. After taking small sips, she seemed to have realized my presence. Abby smiled like a sphinx and playfully hurled the cup at me. She was smiling like some Goddess.

I got up, trying to catch the cup. I realized then how thirsty I was. It would take gallons and gallons of iced water to quench it.

Abeer."

Invidious

"I was waiting for her in her drawing room. Some donation seekers were there. They were waiting for her. They thought me to be one of the donation seekers. They were chit-chatting when one of them casually remarked that Abby may have some underworld contacts, which is why she was so successful in such a short time.

I handed him my card and told him that he would hear from my office for a defamation suit if he stood there for more than five seconds flat.

He ran away. When Abby came down, he was not there. I had to discuss something important. We thought of closing it there. The aroma of freshly brewed coffee could not mask her fragrance. She had not dried her hair. They were tangled, and water was dripping from them.

I pointed out her disheveled hair with my eyes. She smiled and explained. "Oh, they are wet now. It will take almost 35 mins to reach the workplace. It will dry by then; in parking, I will brush." I cannot forget that flowery and earthly smell floating around her, like the smell of the forest after rain. Flawlessly complete and yet waiting and wanting something more.

I felt like taking her in my arms tightly so that her fragrance would infuse in me. I shall never forget this fragrance. Although it has already become a shadow of me, I still long for more.

Pity, I did nothing except see and love her through my eyes. She was blissfully unaware of anything going on inside me.

Abeer."

"Today is my Abby's birthday. This day meant a lot for us, albeit for atypical reasons. She always made it a point to make her birthday extraordinarily special. On this day, she would be so relaxed, free from all her work, she lived a day to its whole.

This year was greatly different. Amid all enjoyment and party, I found Abby distracted. The glow which she had on this day of the year was missing.

Something had caged her spirits.

Nobody else did notice the change. Nobody is expected to. Something is troubling her.

Abeer."

Ihit turned more pages.

"I am right, and I know it in my bones. Something is troubling Abby. I tried to talk to her. But she has buried it deep inside; no way to know what she is hiding unless she lets anybody in. She has, in the past, confided in me. Not this time. She is so touchy these days and easily irritated. The tension of the past weeks is taking a toll on her. She avoids casual outings and fun parties. Instead, she is trying to keep a bold face and pretending nothing is troubling her.

She could fool many. But they do not love her; I do. Whatever the problem, it is eating her alive. She fakes a smile perfectly, but I can see the distance yearning in her eyes. Wish she could trust me enough to tell me.

Today, for some reason, in some context in a customer focus meeting, she said, 'Most of the customers do not express their feelings. But that does not mean they are not there. But, pity, most of us don't understand the difference between indifference and silence.'

What stuck with me was she looked straight at me and asked. Her eyes seemed to have a thin film but were ablaze with anger.

Why was her anger so focused on me, suddenly? Does she think I am ignorant of the difference between her silence and indifference? If I could explain; her unspoken pain is not lost on me.

Abeer."

"I can never forget this date, 30th Dec, Abby called me. She said she wanted to tell me something important. So we met in her office. And my world changed forever.

She said she was going to marry Taksh Saxena in Australia.

She just broke the news in her office in two lines! How could she just leave me? I had never called her to my life. Instead, she came into my life uninvited. She called me her Abeer. Then she tells me that we don't have a future together?

All these months, I kept on waiting. Waiting for Abby to come to me. After being done with all the wait, she said she was going away. Playing with my feeling and my life! I can't think why she did such a thing to me.

Why am I fretting and fuming? She never told me that she loved me. I loved her like crazy, which is why it hurt so much when she said she would marry Taksh.

Would I have felt this bad if she had loved Taksh Saxena and would have decided to marry him? Maybe not!

I feel betrayed and bitter. The feelings that I had is gone. I can not feel anything except this pain. I can't think clearly. I seem to relive those dreaded moments again and again.

She told me about Taksh. All I remember walking out of her office. Was she calling me? I don't know. I could not hear anything. Next, I remember being pulled out of traffic. I walked to the IFFCO chowk. Those who pulled me out of harm's way called a cab and I returned home. My ears are still ringing. And I now ask myself, what exactly do I feel for her, Bitterness, anger, or intense love? I can't even distinguish between them any longer.

Or she has lost her mind after all.

She could not have or would not have forgotten that Abeer belongs to Abby and she is Abeer's. None of us can live without each other.

What'll be her life without me? Nobody else can love her the way I do. How will she live without love? She will die like a fish out of water.

I won't let her go! We belong to each other.

The air I breathe is enriched by her fragrance. My heart echoes with her laughter. Everything will vanish without her. Precisely these are the things that will stop her from going. She must stay here.

Whatever she said or has not said, or the way she told me, I could see the pain when she said she was going forever. I know she loves me madly. I have tangible proof too. I never could muster enough courage to give her the dress I got for her. It was sitting on my desk for ages and then in a forgotten corner of the library in the office, properly gift-wrapped but forgotten as a bad idea. She took it. I realized it when I saw her in that dress at a party where she went as my plus one. All this proves that she loves me. She is my love and won't let her lead a loveless, harsh, and bitter life. Her life should be loaded with love and intense love.

Abeer."

"I came back to add a few lines. Abby has not told me verbatim that she loves me, but her eyes always say it. She looked at me with such a tender, unique, emotional glow. Is it not proof enough that she loves me? It is me who colors her dreams and lightens up her day. It is me who knocks at the door of her eyes when she closes them. How can she live without me? No way! She can't go away. Her whole life is me --- here, and she thinks she can go away. Absurd crazy! Where will she go? It is ONLY me. She would find me all around her wherever she looked.

My arms are her home. In them will she find peace and happiness! Stupid, foolish girl, she says she will go away. How? Her heart is here within mine. Her whole existence is mingled with my breath. Just as I'll die if I stopped breathing, she too would die if she were snatched away from me. I will never do that. I can't let you go, Abby. You are too precious to be lost.

Has she ever thought about what life will be like without me? It is infeasible and never going to happen!

Abeer."

Despair

"*It is crucial that I mention the date here: 31st Dec.*

Time: Evening.

Status: Waiting.

In some time, I would be with Abby. I am prepared. No nervousness or any such feelings. What I still feel is love, perhaps more intensely. Love has become an obsession in the face of its untimely death.

Abeer."

The pencil pressure on the following page was significantly higher than on the previous pages.

"*Date: 31st Dec.*

Time: Night.

Status: Conflicting

I'll narrate a story, the story of an evening; of the events yet to come to pass.

It is the story of Abby. A young woman who saved her father's business and took it to heights. She was a woman who could twist the arms of veterans in her fields but could not see the apparent love. It is also the story of a shy guy, Abeer, who waited and waited for his love to understand his feeling. Abeer, who, for reasons unknown, kept on expecting life to be fair and reciprocate his love with love. He always had challenges with rejections. Growing up among the taunting and bullying crowd brought fewer shades of aggression, inferiority complex, tenacity, and determination. He was always afraid of losing, yet he was determined not to lose.

Tonight would be the most memorable night of his life.

Facing the mirror, he gazed at his reflection for a long time. He was prepared. The old school white shirt and dark grey suit. He had back-brushed his hair. He dabbed a drop white Oudh[16] behind his ears and on his wrist. He was ready. Or thought he was!

He stood there long as if trying to understand what the man in the mirror was saying. His mind was conflicted. Anger and logic were at loggerheads, and he was the man losing the battle on both sides. It was evening. Time to go.

The delivery was late.

He could wait for some more time. He would not be late, and Abby would wait for him. No rush. There was an uneasy calmness in him. Uneasy and frightening.

The flowers he had ordered arrived.

He loaded ice on the champagne bucket and packed it with the bottle of bubbly. It was of the vintage he was saving to use when he proposed to Abby. Though Abby would not taste it, and from

---

[16] *White Oudh - Oud (in Arabic, Oudh) is valued strongly by perfumers for its warm sweetness mixed with woody and balsamic notes. It's an aromatic and complex scent. It is used as oud oil (dehn al oud) or resin (oud mubakhar). Oud is often a base note when used in a perfume composition. Unlike top and middle notes, essential in every perfume, base notes tend to stay on the skin long after the others dissipate. Its woody smell is rich in nuances, ranging from sweet to earthy, with some notes of leather and spices. It depends on the tree species that produces the resin and the technique used for extraction. Oud comes from the wood of the tropical Agar (Aquilaria) tree, a genus that includes 15 different species. The tree is believed to have originated in the Assam region of India and, from there, spread to populate Bangladesh and much of Southeast Asia.*

that day onwards, he too would not, he had planned to just pop the bottle and then gift it to the servers. But that day was now written off from his life. So, there was absolutely no use in saving it. He knew Abby was a teetotaler, but it was the last night together, and he knew Abby would not refuse him if he insisted. Not tonight, their last night together. She owed him that much to share a drink together.

His lips were dry again; he applied lip gel. His lips were drying faster than usual today. As he pocketed the lip gel, his fingers touched another vial. He gripped it.

Still conflicted. The clear liquid in the vial appeared sinister. Should he take it to Abby's farmhouse? Something said it would betray her, yet it felt right at some level.

Abeer knew if the night went as planned, it would be a point of no turning back. So he went back to his study and pulled out the journal. He needed to pen down the story of Abby and Abeer. That should be the befitting end to the story of this night and the final night in this journal.

This is how Abby and Abeer's story came to an end; with their lives.

Abeer"

Ihit took a long breath as he turned a page. Unlike all the previous pages of the journal, the entry was not in black ink. Seemed that Abeer had grabbed anything he could write with. The blue ball pen looked cheaper in comparison. So was the handwriting. The determination of the last page was gone, Abeer's hands were shaking. Between the pages, a lifetime seemed to have passed.

"I never intended to return, but life had an altered ending to the story of Abby and Abeer. It re-wrote the ending in the most brutal manner.

I lived a thousand lives in one night and died as many times.

She was in my arms. Her eyes were getting dreamy. I could not take my eyes off them. Her heaving heart on mine beat as one. I gripped her firmly and drew her closer. She kept on closing her eyes. Music, it always took her to another world. This time, I was in another world too. A world where nothing but love and Abby existed. I had never danced with her before.

Her face, eyes, and movements conveyed what she could never say. Now, I understand there was no need for it. I did fail to understand her then, but today I do, when she is far away.

I had failed her.

Music was picked by Abby. I knew she had it planned to my taste. I could faintly recall what it was. It was just a perfect amalgamation of music, fragrance, and light, yet everything seemed insignificant. My eyes were on Abby as we danced. Each of her movements said how madly and intensely she loved me. For the first time, I could see Abby as a perfect lover. The music playing at its highest notes, and Abby was spinning fast. I wanted to slow her down. It was insane, but that is what Abby is. Seizing the moment, the passion fringing insanity.

I pulled her in my arms again. She smiled a sultry, seductive smile, the first I had ever seen on her. She pulled her loose hair over her head and tilted her head to one side. I saw a drop of sweat roll down from behind her ears through her titling neck to her shoulder blade. I picked it up and tasted it; I am unsure if she noticed it. She closed her eyes and offered her lips. Our love had found each other. Her burning lips, her breath staggering, her heart pounding against mine. She placed my hand on her heart, opened her eyes, and smiled. I grasped her tighter, kissing her fervently, my hand on her heart, trying to clutch it to pacify it.

I felt her hands on my back sliding as I realized the Champagne in her mouth, and she fell. I held her. She was sinking fast. I held her in my arms, realizing with horror; Abby was not breathing. Frantically, I was searching for her pulse. I thought of giving her CPR, but I knew it was too late. She was there on the floor with a smile on her face. My Abby was no more. I could not let her be there on the floor. I picked her up and placed her on the bed. She was sleeping peacefully. No more would she be wrestling between her desires. And yet, this was not what she or I had in our minds for this night. The farmhouse was empty, and the world was still partying with the advent of a New Year.

It took away everything that I had. I drove away, leaving her alone. She was not prepared to reveal me to the world, which is how it shall be. Honoring her wish meant, I cannot follow her. Till the time I complete the work that she has entrusted me with, I have to keep safe us, and our secret.

I am surprised at my calmness now. I am at my home filling the pages of this journal. Why? Abby's and Abeer's love story cannot end with Abeer going to Abby's farmhouse when the end that was planned had changed. The end needs to be told, which is what I am doing. The question that crops up in my mind is not much of why but how. How am I still alive?

Abby is no more, and yet I am living. My heart is numb, but I am still breathing. I don't even know if I am here or if I am still standing at the foot of the bed watching her. I kissed her dead lips, hoping against all sanity that it would wake her up. She believed in the kiss of true love that can breathe life into a dead heart. I kissed her, and she did not wake up.

I am recording my closing entry here. Abby gave life to Abeer; without her, there is no Abeer; and should not be. Abeer dies today.

Abeer."

That was the end of the entries in the journal. Ihit closed the journal. He felt like he had lived two lives through those pages of truth. It was exhausting. He leaned back on his chair, resting his head, his eyes closed, and his heart and mind battling an ethical dilemma.

Part – IV: Truth, Nothing But The Truth

An Announcement

Life by nature is simple; said and unsaid expectations complicate it.

What transpired on the 31st of December was the tipping point of the events that happened a day earlier. Abby had called Abeer in her office. She wanted to tell him that she was leaving the country. Abby could see him walking through the office bay to her cabin. She forgot the lines she had practiced for weeks. There was light in his eyes. He was her Abeer. She took a deep breath.

'Concentrate,' she whispered to herself.

He does not know what Abeer means to me. So, no harm, no foul. What he does not know won't hurt him. She tried to justify soon-to-be actions.

Taking another deep breath, she was mentally getting prepared for any answer or questions that Abeer would pop up.

He was near the door. Abby's preparations felt inadequate.

Smiling, Abeer came in and sat opposite her. He was waiting for her to begin. He always did that; he waited for her to begin.

"I have to go away. Please don't ask me for the details, but I will marry Taksh and settle in Australia. So, I am leaving on 1ˢᵗ Jan. The operation would be taken care of by me remotely from there. So, nothing changes."

Abby's voice betrayed her. It was difficult to talk any further.

What a way to begin the New Year. I wish I had another way, Abeer.

Abeer got up and walked away. Deep in her heart, she knew Abeer had feelings for her and expected him to burst out about his feelings for her. She was prepared for his anger, sarcasm, objection, or blunt refusal. Nothing of that happened. He just got up and went away.

Abby kept sitting, watching him go. She called after him. He kept on walking, not noticing the glass door. He walked through the glass door. It broke into pieces. The shattering sound pulled everyone's attention as they dashed toward the broken door. Abby ran towards him, but he kept on walking. He was oblivious to the broken door, the crowd rushing towards him, Abby calling him. His left knee and right hand, just above the wrist, were bleeding.

Abby stopped at the broken glass door. Abeer had disappeared. People were talking. There would be no end to the speculation, and it no longer mattered. She stood rooted as the realization hit hard. Seeing him walk away, she understood what she had lost. She was so blind to see his love for her. He always stood by her. Why was she battling alone? Regret overwhelmed her. She could have told him about her love for him and her present situation. Together, they would have found a way. She was leaving in 2 days, on 1st Jan wee hours. She first confided in him that she was going away forever. A foreboding was gripping her. Was she too late? She promptly told Irina to take care of the situation and pushed off. She called him. The calls were not answered. A sense of despair hung over her. She immediately sent him a message.

"I am sorry, Abeer. Seeing you walk away, I realize what I have done. I want to talk to you. Allow me to explain. It is important. I know you are angry, and I wish I had done it otherwise, but I messed up. Please come and meet me. Please do it for me. Meet me at my farmhouse tomorrow evening. I promise I will not hurt you anymore."

Abby was relaxed now.

Abeer would read the message. He would understand that I messed up. I should have confided in him. Hope, I am not too late. I will come clean with him tomorrow and enjoy the concluding night of the year the grand way; we deserve to enjoy it. Later, we would connect and plan our way out of this mess.

She drove straight to the farmhouse to make arrangements for the next day.

***

Abeer pulled some cash out of his wallet, paid the cab, and walked in without a word. He was still unable to reconcile what had happened. His Abby was leaving him. He opened the windows, his body scarcely noticing the chilling air of the NCR.[17].

---

[17] *NCR – Near Capital Region – Delhi, Noida, and Gurgaon.*

He stood at the open window gazing vacantly at the trees in his lawn and the blank sky above it. The ugly mark of dark red blood was on him. The bleeding had stopped, and the blood had coagulated, but Abeer was unaware of it all. Abby's words kept on ringing in his ears. He was reliving those moments again and again but was unable to comprehend them. Nothing made sense anymore, his work, his friends, his life.

The maid opened the locked 2nd entrance and did her chores, checking the fridge for the dinner menu. She was surprised to find it Abeer home so early.

"Bhaiya", she called. Her voice was met with no response. Abeer was still lost. She came closer and called again. Abeer did not listen. She shook him a bit gently. "Bhaiya." Abeer turned. To her horror, she saw the blood-soaked clothes on.

"Was there an accident? What happened?"

Abeer looked at her questioningly.

What was she talking about?

He followed her gaze to realize his knee and hand had bled, his clothes were scrapped and soiled with dark red stains. He could faintly remember, like a dream, him walking out of Abby's cabin, a deafening sound behind him as the door crashed.

He mumbled, "Go home. I don't want dinner tonight."

Without waiting for any response, he walked to his bathroom for a shower.

The maid thought of asking why but, looking at Abeer, decided not to talk any further. Instead, she went about cleaning the kitchen and locking the second entrance.

The warm water stung him. He was now painfully aware of numerous minor cuts and bruises. He welcomed it. Anything that would let him take his mind off his meeting with Abby was welcome. It was dark when Abeer realized the past hours were not a dream. He changed and sat in his study, sipping his poison. His eyes were glued to his journal, bound in the finest leather jacket with Abeer engraved in gold.

A ring distracted him no sooner than he had pulled it out. There were missed calls from Adarsh, his assistant; Suresh, his client; and Abby, his love. Then, despite delay, a message from Abby. All of the work could wait till tomorrow. Their world could survive one more night without him. Instinctively he went to Abby's message.

"I am sorry, Abeer. But, seeing you walk away, I realize what I have done."

Sorry for what, Abby, leaving me or breaking my heart in the way you did? You should have realized what you were doing, Abby, before you broke the news. Or was it you never understood my feeling for you, and now you see them loud and clear when it is too late.

"We need to talk. Let me explain." The message continued.

Explain what you have done and why you have done it? That's it. You don't want to tell me it was a mistake and you are not going away?

"It is important. I know you are angry, and I wish I would have done it otherwise, but I messed up."

Was I ever important to you? You should have done it differently. You should have trusted me with whatever was bothering you for months. But you choose to go away. Instead, you opted to lead a life of compromise and unhappiness. You, indeed, have messed up your and my life.

"Meet me. Please do it for me, in my farmhouse tomorrow evening."

Has it ever happened that I did not reach out to you whenever you called me? I will meet you. This time is not for you. I need closure too. I will do this for myself. I always had selflessly loved you. Your betrayal has broken my heart, and I owe it to myself to get answers.

"I promise I will not hurt you anymore."

Yes, I promise you will not hurt me anymore.

Abeer blocked his calendar for the 31st of Dec. He would spend night of the year with Abby! A lot was going on in his mind.

He pulled out the journal and started writing.

A Realization

At dusk, Abeer's car entered the farmhouse. House did not exhibit any sign of any life as far as he could see. A note on the table read, "I am freshening up. Will join you shortly."

Abby had taken care of the arrangements tonight. Cerulean blue walls with large bay windows. From the window hung blue satin curtains with white laces. In the middle of the room hung a huge chandelier and two mini chandeliers on both sides. In the vase were white roses, white lilies, and white jasmine, with two stands of night jasmine in each of the vases. She loved white flowers, and night jasmine was her favorite.

Abeer looked at the bouquet he was carrying, red and black roses with two strands of night jasmine. He kept them at the center table and sat waiting for Abby while rehearsing his plan in his mind.

I am Abeer. I am in control. Wait till Abby comes in. Smile and hide your pain. Listen to all the useless explanations that she would give. I would not confront her. It's futile. If she has not yet understood me till now, what is the use of telling her. I would listen to her and then I would ask her to make this day memorable for me. A drink and a dance that is all I ask for, and she would not deny me that. We will share a drink. That would be her first and last drink. Both Abby and Abeer will die tonight.

Abeer unscrewed the cork. He took out a vial of a transparent liquid, methylenedioxymethamphetamine, and added it to the bottle of Champagne. He allowed it to mix slowly, screwed the cork back, and let it chill on ice.

Many things were playing on Abeer's mind, his love and her betrayal. He had never asked anybody anything in his life. He was not going to change that today. He steered away from any confrontations in his personal life. He avoided conflict at the cost of any amount of money. He seldom had any expectations from anyone. Abby was the first person he had expectations from. He expected her to understand him, his love, and his silence.

Abeer heard a click, and the door was opened. It was Abby's room. Abeer had a full view of the room from where he was sitting. It had minimal furniture, and three walls were made of mirrors, creating an illusion of space. The dressing table with one set of chairs faced the bed. Again, care was taken to select linen. It was pure silk, like a sheet of light blue. There were five cushions and giant pillows with fur blankets at the foot of the bed. Abby smiled at Abeer. She was about to step out when a mobile bell rang.

"AV here," the walls of the empty house echoed her voice carrying it to Abeer.

"Yes, I don't want to be disturbed…."

She had stepped in a bit.

"Yeah … something personal…I understand."

Abeer tried to advert his gaze, but he could not. He had seen her a thousand times, but today she looked different. She looked so different! She looked a tired but relaxed, like she had fought a war and now had returned home. The red dress clung tightly to her waist with a jewel. The slit at her arms fell from her left hand holding the cell. She seldom wore jewelry except for some special occasions. Abeer smiled to himself.

Jewelry! What is the special occasion - Farewell or Confession?

Studs in her ears sparked with brilliance. A big solitaire rested just above the cut of her plunging neckline, but those were not what held Abeer's attention. His eyes were fixed on her face. She looked calm and confident. Her eyes were solemn, her finger deftly tapping on the mobile.

I love her. I can't do this. I can't let her go without a fight. I am not clear about what her problems are, and I will never know them. If she cannot take that first step, I would. I need to. I can't expect her to act on something that I have never said. Maybe, the way I had been waiting for her to reciprocate, she was waiting for me.

"Ihit will take care of those. Just ensure the papers are sent today...." Her voice wandered to Abeer. She was not tense but seemed to be explaining some essential things. There was always something that needed her attention.

There was always something contesting for her attention. Maybe, she wanted from someone for a change. I, too, became one of all the others. How was I special to her if I treated her like others? I never told her how special she was to me. I remained wrapped up in my own world, and even with all my love for her, I failed to see her. I failed to see her struggle with the basic need of life, love.

"I will be in constant touch. Ha ha ha... I would be doing the afternoon shift to be with you all."

Destiny is written. She is going. What more could happen? The worst is already written. It could not be any worse; just better. I have a duty to look beyond myself and be a superior man. I would confront her. We will find a solution for anything she is troubled with. This time, the onus is mine to take that first step. This murder-suicide is a ridiculous plan. I should not have been so quick in letting my love go away without even one fight. It is insane to kill my love and myself when I have not expressed my love or tried to fight for it.

"Hope you got it all. Okay. Take care. Will talk to you later, in a brand-new year. Bye."

Silly me! I am not going to ask her to share a drink with me. Instead, while going, I will take the bottle of Champagne and flush it down the drain.

Abeer felt pleasanter about his decision. It had lifted a heavy burden from his heart.

Abby switched on the music system. Light instrumental filled the room from above. The carved wooden cabinet was specially created for the special effect. Above it was another cabinet filled with books. She took a brief look in the mirror before stepping out to the living room. Suddenly, she checked the smell on her wrist. She dabbed a bit on her wrist and her neck.

Abeer swallowed hard.

The deep red frock complimented her glowing skin. Two flaps casually hung from her shoulders were ready to slide down whenever she gave them a slight moment. The hair parted on the left side was left open. Some locks fell on her high determined forehead and brow. How gravely he wanted to pull her towards him, embrace her, kiss her, and cover her perfectly in his arms so that she'll forget the rest of the world.

His eyes fell on the bottle. It wasn't required anymore. He picked it up and looked around for the kitchen. The kitchen was just after the dining space, a little beyond the living room. He quickly dashed to the kitchen, kept the bottle in a corner, and returned to the sofa just in time for Abby to turn.

Abby stood at the door of her room, watching him quietly. He searched for words but again failed. Was she Abby? No, she was his Abby. Abby, he always loved to see. She was smiling at him as she turned towards him. It was a smile that he had never seen. She came closer to him. He could vividly smell that earthly smell of the first rain in the forest.

For a moment, he was lost as to where to start. But he knew he had to. He cleared his throat and took her hand. He knew that after a few hours, those soft hands he was holding would slip away from him forever. Yet, he got to take a chance.

What if she refused to see his point? Would he ever be able to leave them with poise?

A Transformation

A day earlier

Abby had realized Abeer's love for her. It struck her as she saw him walk through the glass door and disappear. Though she always knew them a day earlier, she knew how deep it was. It was a mistake letting such love go. So she had messaged Abeer to meet her on the 31st at the farmhouse.

Abby had asked Neer to arrange the farmhouse for the 31st, with a specific set of linen and drapes, and asked him to take off as soon as work gets over by afternoon or late afternoon.

Abby reached the farmhouse a not much later than Neer had left. She had picked up some flowers. Abby wanted to give the farmhouse her touch. She arranged them in a vase. The incident of yesterday playing in her mind.

There was easier way to save Cena Cosmica than what I have planned. Then I was a fool and stupid not to take the help of the man who loves me. Instead, I wrote a script to make my life miserable, blamed fate and played the victim. I am not a victim, and I am somewhat surprised as to why I did choose this martyr's way. Years of struggle and fighting for each win had made me tired, and I tried taking the easy way. I am not a victim. I had fought, survived, and again will do so. I am AV. I will save my Cena Cosmica and my love. I want them both, and that is not up for any negotiations. Not anymore.

She had picked up a red dress from Ambi Mall yesterday. It was unlike any dress that she had worn earlier. Elegant and raunchy with slits that opened till a quarter of the thighs under the flares. The belt could hold a jeweled pin she had picked up from Gold Souk this morning. Her heart was racing. She would initiate such events tonight from where there would be no going back.

She was pleased that she had dismissed the staff for the day except Neer, but he had left when she came in. This was the most decisive day of her life, and she needed absolute privacy. Coconut water was nicely stocked in the fridge, and the jelly she had prepared had settled well. She wanted to bake a cake, but that would be tedious. Neer quietly slipped into his quarters unnoticed. He had lost all his money. He returned to dig into the reserve money he had planned to send for his child's fees. He knew he would slip in, take the money and slip out. No one would know.

Abby wanted time to stop and run at the same time. She was waiting for Abeer and dreading his arrival too. It was time for Abeer to come. He was never late. Today, he was. She had both butterflies and a sinking feeling in the pit of her stomach.

The doorbell rang. It was 4:18 pm. Abby rushed to open it, thinking it was Abeer. It was Shay, not Abeer!

"You bitch, you have no right to my life. You cannot dictate who I date."

"True," Abby replied in a cold voice.

"Then stop whatever you are doing. I am serious about Mahira."

"Say that to Hinal." She replied with a taunt.

Emotions were flaring.

"Abby, please consider your decision. Can't you see nobody is okay with this decision? You are ruining our lives. Don't play a God."

"I don't sell candies. I can't keep everybody happy. But I know what is to be done, and I have made up my mind."

"You can, and nobody dares stand up to you."

"Because I am right."

"No, because they are afraid of you. We are afraid that something will change your mood, and we will be penniless. We all are living under the shadow of fear."

"Then do as I say, cousin Shay."

"Shit! Damn it! Abby, damn you! How can you be so cold?"

"I am not cold; you are cold and heartless, Shay. How conveniently have you forgotten that a girl went into trauma just because of you? She was a train wreck. She had a nervous breakdown; she was thrown out of her hostel. None of the colleges would give her admission. Such was the stigma. She could not face any interview for a job. You ruined her life, Shay. I will not let you do it again."

"I can explain it, Abby. We had a 'no commitment relationship.' We were free to walk away without consequences or guilt whenever we liked. We both agreed, but then she wanted more from the relationship. I don't like to be chained. I tried to tell her, but she kept on clinging to me. She tried to chain me. I had to break it. It wasn't a relationship that I had committed for life."

"So, break it again. It should be easy for you. Now that you have experience."

"What is it? Some kind of twisted revenge. I told you with Mahira, it is different."

"If you genuinely love her so much, break all your relationship with me and marry her. Take care of your responsibilities. Can you do that? No, as much as I know you, all you want to do is flirt and spend the money I earn."

"You are just making everything about you. Stop all this nonsense about guilt and responsibility?"

"Have you forgotten Shay? Hinal was my friend; you met her through me. I did not intervene then as I thought you both were mature adults who could take care of yourselves. I had no idea that Hinal would be in such a fragile state. Once you broke her heart, it broke her wholly. Again, you are repeating the history with Mahira. You met her at my party and started flirting with her. Why do you have to hunt for your next prey from my guest list? It is cheap. I would not let you destroy her life too."

"I am not the psycho that you are making me. You know well enough, Abby, this time it is different."

"Oh really! How is Mahira dissimilar from Hinal? To what extent can you go for Mahira? Can you leave everything for her? Your father can fall for this act, but not me. Shay, you will never change, not for Hinal and not for Mahira."

"You have got father turned against son. My father would not dare annoy you; that might jeopardize his precious project. You should remember this, dear cousin; blood is thicker than water. Do not try to break us apart. Step aside from the matter that is not yours to be involved in, or else you will be responsible for anything that happens to you."

Neer was hearing everything. He thought he would step in, but then he would be asked why he was on the premises. It was embarrassing for him to confess that he had lost all his salary on gambling with heavy liquor on his breath. So he kept on peeping from his window.

It is their personal matter, he reasoned to himself.

"Get out of my face, Shay. I want some peace and quiet."

Murmuring under his breath, Shay turned to leave. He passed a heavy vase near the door; he saw a perfect opportunity. He meant to hurt Abby.

"I will kill anybody who stands between Mahira and me." He declared as he hurled the heavy brass vase at her. Luckily his aim was sloppy. It missed Abby. And Shay walked away.

Abby had a bottle of coconut water to calm her down. This episode with Shay was unexpected. She was glad that Abeer was not there. It was 4:50 pm. Abeer was late. Pacing up and down in the front lawn was of no use. She needed to compose herself. Washing her hair and blow drying always helped. She went in again, leaving the front door open.

Seizing that moment, Neer slipped off from the property with all the money had collected to send home.

Abby had finished blow-drying her hair when she heard Abeer enter the hall. Never had she felt this nervous. She started doing her hair, hoping it would calm her down. Today, it was of little help. It was the time. She was about to leave the room she was saved by the phone bell. Talking business took her mind off the nervousness. She was prepared for a latest venture in her life and to include Abeer in it.

An Understanding

Abby stood at the door of her room, watching him quietly. She was dressed up for him. She had been waiting for him and now standing so close to him. Till yesterday, holding his hand looked like a dream; now he was her's. His white musk had enveloped her. His eyes were sharp but reddish. It seemed he had not slept; a strange smile was still on his lips. A smile made of pain and determination. Abby felt like touching his 5 o'clock shadow but refrained. She had the whole night for it. But first, she needed to come clean.

Her eyes had a strange light, and equally mysterious was her smile. She crept closer to Abeer, within his breath. Abeer's senses were filled with her; she smelled of a lush green forest, washed after a fresh rain.

Abeer had to talk to her. Fight for his love. He needed help figuring out where to start. Clearing his throat, he lightly took her hand. He took a chance. He was not convinced if Abby would see his point. He was unsure if he would be able to graciously accept her decision. Yet, Abeer knew he would need to talk to her. Otherwise, after a few hours, those soft hands he was holding would slip away from him forever.

Abeer heard something. It was Abby's voice.

"Abeer, I love you. I loved you since I knew what love was, and in the church, I knew it was you. I am sorry I waited for so long to tell you this. I should have done this earlier."

Abeer was surprised, not expecting Abby to confess her love, at least not tonight.

Why is Abby doing this? And now, of all the time, merely a few hours when she has planned to go away. What is in her mind? Is this just a confession, or is she changing her mind about going?

"You mean you are not going to Australia?" Abeer asked cautiously.

He had planned to tell her about his feelings, but she came forward with hers. A ray of hope kindled that she would stay back.

"No, I have to."

"I do not understand. Is there something you want of me?"

"Trust."

"That I have given you aplenty. It's time; you trust me."

"It was my mistake to not share it with you sooner. Trust was never a concern. I was tired of fighting. I was about to surrender without a fight. I had forgotten, I have you. I need you to get my love and purpose in my life."

Abeer nodded and wrapped his arm around her shoulder. Abby related the whole story of the Australian ties, the deal with Taksh, the completion of the projects, and getting Cena Cosmica's shares back from them. Abeer listened to Abby without a word.

"When I was about to tell you about my feeling, Taksh told me about his plan to liquidate their shares. I felt betrayed by fate. With the hard work I had put in, I thought I was now entitled to a accomplished life. I had forgotten that life is seldom fair. I was bitter and became kind of suicidal. I had forgotten who I was. And that afternoon, when you walked away, I realized I want it all in my life."

"I am in. What's the plan?"

"I was not confident at the moment. I was under the assumption that once I marry Taksh, I have to sever ties with you. I don't have to. I am marrying him to save Cena Cosmica. I don't love him. I love you, and I will always do. Is there any point in severing our relationship? Rather, on the eve of my departure to get married to a man I purely have business interest with, I would like to take our relationship to another level."

"A long-distance relationship?"

"If that is okay with you."

"Can I come over?"

"Yes. I will keep visiting the city. My Cena Cosmica is here. I always have a reason to visit, at least once a month. This farmhouse would be our home then."

"Wow! That sounds so much not like you."

"Once I realized the secrets of my heart, I transformed."

Abeer sat looking at Abby. He was at a loss for words. He had thought he would need to plead with her to stop, convince her of his love, and here she was, Abby, as usual, changing the whole narrative.

Abby looked at him with questions in her eyes. Then, suddenly, something struck Abby.

"Abeer, but I can't promise that I would not have any physical relationship with Taksh. Right now, I know or trust him little to tell him that this relationship will end as soon as his project takes off and my shares are back with me. Too much is at stake for me. I can't be this transparent with him as I am with you."

"As long as you don't love him, I am okay. Who you sleep with is not my concern. Your heart is mine, and that is what I refuse to share."

Abby heaved a sigh of relief. Abeer pulled her closer.

"If you had told this earlier, I would not have gone crazy thinking if you ever loved me or not. You would not have suffered in silence. There would not be a pain in your eyes." Gently he kissed her closed eyes.

"I would have arrested the glow on your cheeks, never let it dull." She felt his lips on her cheeks.

"I would not have let the smile disappear from your lips." He continued. This time, his lips were close to her. His white Oudh was filling her up. Her lips parted, and she felt his moist lips on her, haltingly taking her lips in his with sweet patience and intense love.

Time flew. They, at last, found themselves in each other. Abby could not believe the night she dreaded was turning out to be the best night of her life. A call on Abby's mobile distracted them. It was her travel agent with update. She stepped aside to the kitchen to take the call. In the hall was her dream which should not be interrupted.

The call was 2-3 minutes. Walking into the kitchen, Abby's eyes caught a bottle of Champagne.

Abeer knows I don't drink. So then, why did Abeer get it? Was he going to tell me about his feeling? I blurted out. As usual, I did not give him any chance to talk.

She stood there fidgeting with the bottle's cork.

Why did he get it and keep it here? Was it a farewell gift, and he just could not give it? It was too painful for him. Well, he was unaware of my feelings or plans then. Now he knows. I am glad he is with me. How much has life changed in just 24 hours? And how much it would change? Tomorrow will bring in a novel life, innovative rules, a fresh playbook.

Abby unscrewed the cork.

What the hell! Why not make one change for this beautiful night, a drink to celebrate my intimacy with Abeer and a unexperienced relationship with him. So tonight, I would mark a pristine me.

Daintily, she took a sip, not bad, but tonight, she won. She swigged more. The taste appealed a bit more. She gulped some more.

This is a big night. A newfound phase of my life begins. I am going to marry Taksh, but tonight I will be in the arms of my love. I will be loved, I will be loved, and I will be love's bride.

She drank a bit more.

Tonight, the taste of my fist kiss lingers not merely on my lips, but on my soul.

She drank a some more. A tingling sensation raced through her. Then, keeping the bottle away, she returned to her love, her Abeer.

An Inadvertence

Abby felt lighter. A tingling sensation in her limbs and a lightness in her heart were new. A giggle escaped her lips. December appeared warmer, and yet she needed the warm embrace of Abeer. Abeer was still in the hall waiting for her. She got his hand and led him to her room to the recliner, and she sat on the edge of the bed. Abeer looked around; the mirror was all around. Abeer never understood her obsession with mirrors when she seldom looked at them. Abby was smiling. He knew the fleeting time that would snatch these precious moments away. Their next meeting would be somewhat unique, in constrained time, out and hidden from prying eyes. Still, it was more than enough that she was, is, and will always be in his life as his love.

Abby was pursing her lips; they looked a bit parched. Abeer smiled and went to the fridge to pick up a bottle of apple juice. She took a sip from the bottle and passed it to him. He took a swig or two. Tardily, she took the bottle away from his hand, kept it on the side table, and offered her hand. Abeer followed her lead and, in the softest voice, asked, "Abeer, will you dance with me ... tonight, now?"

Abeer nodded.

Abby smiling, changed the music and nodded. Captivatingly she came near him; Abeer drew her closer, wrapping his hands around her waist. Her hand was on his, and another was on his shoulder. The soft, graceful melody continued, and two figures sailed in the air, floating like a feather in the gentle breeze of winter.

All along, Abeer was watching her eyes, unblinking, they were his world, and for the first time, they reciprocated his love. The music grew intense, and he could feel Abby breathing deeply. Her heart raced with his. He gripped her firmly and drew her still closer, tighter his hands around her waist. He began gaining momentum.

Pink lines of dreams began emerging in Abby's eyes. It was getting difficult for her to keep her eyes open. Still, she matched his steps. Abby loved dancing and dancing like she had never danced before. But this dance was different; she was dancing with him. She was dancing like she was in a dream.

Her breath became more rapid, eyes getting deeper and deeper into the mystery zone. Abeer felt like kissing those dreamy yet open eyes with all the love he had. A color of intensity was reflected on her face as her legs moved faster and faster. He, too, was, in a way, guiding her movements, urging them to move faster and faster, caught up in the moment.

Abeer pulled her in his arms closer, refusing to allow space between them. Abby read his mind; she felt tipsy and warm, her lips yearning for his. She wanted him, his lips on her, raining on her searing body. Exposing her nape, she pulled her hair over her head. The cool air on her nape felt good. Abby knew his breath smelt nice; she invited him, lips parted, eyes closed.

Her lips were burning, his heart pounding, his grasp tighter. His kisses were becoming wilder and more intense. Finally, she wanted him to tear open that red dress, and she placed his hand on her bosom. He was pleased to comply, but then his heart tried to kiss her for a bit longer.

A moment more, just a moment more. Let me kiss you for a moment more. The whole night is ours. My lips have been thirsty for years; they need a bit more.

It was the height of intensity and music playing at its highest notes; Abby was whirling faster and faster. Abeer's eyes were not able to catch her movements. And then his world stopped. She stopped and fell. Abeer swiftly caught her in his arms. He could not comprehend for a moment what had happened. Abby was not responding. He kept on calling out her name.

His throat was now dry. As he pursed his lips, he noticed the taste of Champagne. His breath stopped in dread. He had dismissed that taste on his lips.

He called her out louder. But, again, she was silent, non-responsive, and not breathing.

Abeer could not imagine how on earth could Abby drink the poisoned Champagne. He had discarded the suicide-murder plan and had kept away the bottle. He ran to the kitchen to check. The bottle was half empty.

How could Abby drink it? She was a teetotaler!

He felt lost. It was wrong. Abby could not die. Fearfully, he thought, of administering CPR. In a moment, it dawned upon him that it is of no use and would leave forensic evidence. He sat there weighing all the options.

Shall I confess? Who would believe that it was an accident? I had an intent; I got the bottle. Nobody would believe me. It would be for the best. Without Abby, I have no reason to live. It is decent this way. I will confess. Or shall I just empty the bottle? I would reunite with Abby.

Abeer sat with Abby in his arms, looking at her and his decisions for and of his life. Every option seems lucrative. The gaping hole and pain he felt with Abby collapsing in his arms were beyond his endurance. His eyes were dry, and his heart howled.

Then something struck him. He pulled himself together. He had work to do. Methodically, he rubbed off the traces of his presence from the entire house. He bagged the bottle and the flowers he got and rubbed off all the places he had touched. Then he took her in his arm, laid her on her bed, removed her shoes, and placed it conscientiously on the side of the bed. His Abby appeared to be sleeping peacefully.

Abeer switched on the AC to full blast. 'Elysian,' he whispered as he turned off the lights.

Leaving her alone, Abeer drove away, dumping the bottle and flowers on the footpath near sector 31 and another in sector 43.

A Damnation

Hours had passed since Ihit had closed the journal. So, much has happened in the preceding months. He had lost a friend and had saved a man who despised her. Ihit did not even have enough time to grieve a loss. He had work to do. The work that Abby had assigned him. She still needed him to do one final thing. He looked at his watch; Taksh would be calling any minute. One work to be done, and then he could say goodbye to Abby.

Taksh came late to Ihit's house. Ihit avoided meeting his clients at his home and so late, but Taksh was special. He needed to finish one task he had held for a long time. He pulled out Abby's will. She had made him the sole executor of the will. Along with that was a letter.

"I know this is weird, but it is needed. Though you would not need to execute my will for a long time, here it is. I have trained Bahar well as my intern. She is ready. With Bhallaji's supervision, she should be able to take care of Cena Cosmica. She believed in this impossible dream, and after me, if anybody needs to live this dream, it is her. There is an arrangement with Taksh about Cena Cosmica. Hopefully, by the time you would get to execute my will, that arrangement will no longer be required. Still, I need to let you in on that in case I am not so lucky. Just ensure I am remembered and Cena Cosmica is still the same. Cena is my baby, save her and nurture her. Rest of my properties, insurance, etc. I leave it to you to do as you see fit, except you give it to those

of my relatives who have done nothing more than hurt me and my family time and again ."

Ihit had got this will in the first week of January. She mailed it to the concierge on 31st December. Revealing her will have meant showing her arrangement with Taksh and, worse, people knowing that Abby was not the sole owner of Cena Cosmica. It meant too much to her to bring that kind of scrutiny to the court case. He had sent it to a lab to ascertain of no forgery. It had to have an alibi not to use the will in the court case. The lab result came as the court case reached the hearing date.

Taksh was sitting comfortably when Ihit came in with all the papers. So he handed Ihit some papers.

"I have transferred all our shares of Cena Cosmica to you, Mr. Basu. Hope you have the cash and bonds ready." Taksh asked.

Ihit nodded. He went through all the papers as finishing act. He knew what was in it and had drafted it, but before signing, it was important to ensure everything again.

Ihit smiled and handed Taksh cash and bonds.

"I still don't understand Mr. Basu; if Abby had this money, she could have brought back her shares from me. Why did she not do that long ago? She always wanted to be the sole owner of Cena Cosmica. Instead, she got associated with my project to get my shares. I fail to understand this."

"This is her insurance money. Her father had taken insurance for her, and she added some more when she took some mortgage for renovation. What fell short got covered by her saving and her jewelry. Cena Cosmica was her life, and I intend to keep it that way as the executor of her will." Ihit replied dryly.

"Since the business is concluded, I would take your leave. I am once again sorry for your loss."

"Me too."

Taksh left. Cena Cosmica's papers were with Ihit. One thing was left, he recalled with pleasure. Read out the will to the family. He had asked them for a meeting which they agreed. They liked and trusted him after Shay's case.

Bijlee, Shay, and Dr. Divyansh's world fell apart. They had high hopes that they would become the trustee and do as they liked with Abby's money. They had even planned to sell off Cena Cosmica to the highest bidder. But, in moments, they were left penniless.

"Forgery!" Shay said with anger.

"I have a certificate proving it is not. All due diligence has been put in place. The court, too, agrees with the will getting in force."

"She ruined us. All our lives, we lived with the fear that she would cut us off in her will, and we tried to appease her but to what end. She left us penniless." Wailed Bijlee.

"You all ruined her life, yet she took you in as charity. You deserve what came to you. I am sad that she had to die for you to get what you deserve."

Shay was about to hit Ihit, but Ihit ducked and, in a quick reflex, punched him in the face, knocking him out.

Dr. Divyansh was silent and held Shay back when he tried to attack again.

"This property is mine to take care of now. I want all of you out of here in a minute. Since Abby tolerated you, I give you 20 days to move back to your ancestral home that Abby's father gave up. She, too, had given up her claim on it. Go there and try to be human beings."

Abby's so-called family was fretting and fuming, cursing her and her mother.

The next stop was Cena Cosmica. It was 11:00 pm. It was peak hours for the restaurant-chain's office. He was acting fast, like a man on a mission. All the paperwork was done; he needed to communicate it to the staff tonight.

Ihit had drawn an elaborate plan. Abby's properties were to be liquidated except Cena Cosmica. The amount was to be put into a trust that would take care of the administration and management of Cena Cosmica. With him in the faith would be Bahar Sadaf and Sanjay Bhalla, two individuals who got associated with Abby since the beginning. Bahar had joined her as an apprentice, just out of college. Sanjay Bhalla was recruited by her father and was trusted by him explicitly.

Though the news of Abby's death was received with teary eyes by Cena Cosmica, all of them promised to keep Abby's legacy going on. A few months back, Ihit had asked them to continue in consistent fashion as it was with Abby. He asked them to trust him. He had Abby's will, but revealing it would have been detrimental to the ongoing investigation. They agreed to cooperate; things went on as if Abby was there, till Ihit read her will to the family and friends, and her colleagues from Cena Cosmica.

Ihit's work was done.

It was almost 2:00 am when Ihit retired to bed. He had slept a wink. He felt someone sobbing. He opened his eyes, and in the dim light of the night, he could make out a shadow standing near his table. The shadow was looking down at the journals.

Ihit stopped his approach. Perhaps, he knew who the shadow was. Instinctively, his hand clutched a slight bundle tied as a pendant to a silver chain hanging from his neck and reaching his mid-abdomen. It always remained hidden from the eyes of others, under his shirt. Ihit pulled out the bundle. It contained a lock of Abby's hair and a vial. The vial was half empty. It contained

methylenedioxymethamphetamine.

He felt the shadow, smiling, touching the gold letters Abeer.

Ihit's thoughts flew to Abby when she left for Australia on 5th Nov, two years ago.

"I would miss you, Abby," Ihit said.

"No, Ihit, you would not miss me after seeing the gift I have kept in your car. It'll keep you occupied. You will feel as if I am close to you."

In his car, Ihit found a journal with a name embossed in gold, 'Abeer.'

It was a puzzle to him why would Abby, who always called him Ihit, present him with a blank journal with the name 'Abeer'. His mind raced to possible answers, but his heart knew. He knew it was for him and for reasons best known to Abby. She had named him Abeer. She had given him a new identity.

From that day, Ihit kept writing till the 31st of Dec, he kept sharing all his love, passion, and obsession with his new signature, 'Abeer'. What Ihit never knew till the previous night together how important Abeer was to Abby.

Ihit had longed for Abby's love, never realizing that he was her Abeer, the love of her life, since the time she understood what love was.

If Ihit had told Abby how he had felt about her, maybe…maybe Abby would have said to him that he, Ihit was her Abeer; perhaps she would have trusted him with her plans earlier, and that night of 31st December never happened.

Every day and night, the whirlpool of What Ifs kept tormenting him. Every 'What If' indicated that Abby could be alive.

Tears welled up in his eyes. He knew the shadow. The shadow of Abby smiled and disappeared.

Pain clutched his existence and he brought out the vial. All his work was done. He could take a swig and join Abby forever. He sat down in his chair.

That's it! Just do it. His heart whispered.

He smelled the lock of hair. Familiar earthly smell. His Abby's smell. The room was filled with the freshness of the morning. His Abby was waiting.

In a moment, all the pain will be gone. His heart insisted. He opened the vial. Pressed it to his lips.

"The accused, Ihit Basu, is hereby found guilty of intent." A forceful voice rang in his ears.

"It is true that Ihit Basu did not offer Abby Champagne. He had changed his mind at the last minute and had dumped the bottle in the kitchen. But he went there with the purpose of killing. He had all the intent and almost followed through with the act. Now, he wants to eliminate the pain of living without his love. He is a coward. He is guilty on two counts of murder, Abby and Abeer." Abeer's voice was booming in his ears like an echo in an empty courtroom.

"Yes, I have been killed too. Abby brought me to existence, and this person kept denying his heart and avoided talking to her about his feeling. He kept on suffocating me and my feeling. My life looks worthless. Abeer lived for Abby. I was Abeer for her. When she is no more, what is Abeer? Where is he now? Where am I now? I am no more. This man denied my love and I died with my love, Abby. There is no Abeer without Abby. With her death, Abeer, too, is lost forever. You killed me, Ihit Basu. You killed both Abby and me."

"Ihit Basu, how would you plead? Do you think you are innocent and it was all an accident? If you had not brought that vial, Abby and I would have been here."

Ihit looked at the edge of the table where Abby's shadow had disappeared. Abeer was standing there, like a ghost, watching him. Seemed as if she could see Abeer prosecuting Ihit.

"I plead guilty on both accounts." Ihit's lips trembled as words slid between his teeth.

Abeer continued, "How would you sentence yourself? You are the judge, and you are the jury."

"I would accept any sentence you give me. Give me the death penalty, Abeer. I will gladly join Abby. I want to. I can't live like this, dying a thousand death every day. Carrying the burden of what I know secretly. Free me from this pain. Give me a death sentence."

"How can I, Ihit? Remember, I am just a representation of the love that Abby created long before she saw you. When she realized you were me, she handed over the journal to you, making my life a responsibility of yours. Yet, I died when Abby died. I am a victim here. Give me justice. Don't ask me to relieve you from your pain. I ask you to be fair to Abby and me." Abeer said. His figure glided over the ground.

Ihit was silent, looking at the translucent image in the form of Abeer. He knew what was to be done. He was mustering enough courage to go through it. He drew a long breath and, with a forced calm voice, said.

"For the heinous crime that Ihit committed, not trusting his love, hiding his feeling, unrealistic expectation, and unforgivable act of getting methylenedioxymethamphetamine for a murder-suicide, I find Ihit guilty. His act resulted in the accidental consumption of the poison. Although, when she danced, Ihit did not suspect something was odd. He kept on living it as a dream. In her dying breath, he did not even confess to what he had done. He kept looking at her, indecisive about telling her the truth or letting her slip into eternal sleep in peace. Ihit Basu, for your crimes, you are at this moment sentenced to LIFE. You will live a painful, loveless life. Death would free you, so now, Ihit Basu, you are to live. Life is your punishment."

Ihit sentenced himself, biting his lips ferociously. A droplet of blood oozed on his lips as he looked at Abby's diaries and his journal with Abeer written in gold.

Characters

Main Cast

Abhishikta Vats

Jai Prakash Chautala – Inspector

Abeer – Abby's love

Ihit Basu – Lawyer

Shay Vats - Abby's Cousin

Relatives:

Siddharth Vats – Abby's father

Bijlee Vats – Aunt

Dr. Divyansh Vats– Abby's Uncle

Police:

Hari Krishna – Constable

Mona Kuttan – Colleague of Jai

Narender Agarwal – DSP

Biz Contacts

Vivaan Khatri – Owner of another chain of restaurant

Asreet Kaur – Journalist

Shabbir Amin – Siddharth's Advocate

Dr. Rubina Ahmed – Assistant HOD of Psychology, State Medical College

Jeet – Sidharth's friend

Taksh – Jeet's son

Varsha – Jeet's wife

Others:

Irina D'Costa – Personal Assistant of AV

Neer – Caretaker

Mahira Sanya – Painter, Shay's love interest and Abby's friend

Hinal Shah – Shay's ex-girl friend and Abby's friend

Kyra – Abby's school friend

Falak – Neighbor - Bride

Prisha – Abby's dance friend

Other Titles

Heir – End of Innocence

Padmakishori was married to a man older than her father to save her kingdom, Gavpundir from imminent civil war and to give Jodhgarh an heir. Her husband refused to share his heart with her. For him, she was just a means to provide his kingdom with an heir. Padmakishori is faced with a dilemma – to accept a life without love and passion or to walk the dangerous path of lies and secrecy to fulfil her bodily desires. She picks up the path of secrecy, something that Garvpundir was very familiar with. One after another Padma learns the bloody past, present and foreseeable future of the kingdom. Will Padma understand the stir Tamira created with her free spirit that plunged generations to come in fear of yet another coup? Is Roop justified to snatch away the love and passion of young hearts for patriotism and politics? Will Uday ever find out what his wife yearned for? Will Padma understand the riddle of the soothsayer to give the kingdom an heir or will she be caught and executed for treason?

https://www.amazon.in/dp/9389600928

Heir – Dawn of Deception

Dawn of Deception is the final part of Heir. Padma yearning continues as she tries to adapt to the life and palace in Jodhgarh. Her soul rebelling as injustice that fate had written for her.

From the heart of mountains to barren desert, Heir is her journey from a naïve princess to the Queen she never thought she would be.

What would Padmakishori, a princess of 16 years, was married off to a man older than her father but a powerful king to give both the kingdom of Jodhgarh and Garvpundir an heir, do?

Trapped in a loveless marriage, how will she change the fate written for her?

What does the future hold for Roop; the Queen who cared more for the Crown than her love. How did Tamira - who lurked in the shadows change Padmakishori?

What did the soothsayer see in the river of future?
Will Virsa ever forget his first love?
Will Uday ever give Padmakishori the love she deserved?
Will history get repeated with Devdan?

An erotic political thriller that spans across 4 generation and 2 kingdoms.

https://www.amazon.in/dp/9390542286

Ruby Drops

Amazon Best Seller in Poetry section, with 4.5 out of 5 rating with more than 52 reviews.

Ruby Drops is not an anthology of poems. They are cries of soul and happiness dropped from eyes as tears. They are witness to flights of freedom and testimony of shackles. Life is but a rainbow, made of smile and tears, so are the Ruby Drops. These are feeling of a girl growing up. It has elements of fairy tales, the Prince Charming, to monsters to facing the reality of life. It is a journey of smiles and tears.

Ruby Drops is also a story of struggle against depression in the form of poems. It helped me to heal. It is a part of my soul and soul is not for sale. Every cent of profit from Ruby Drops is pledged to Random Acts to help prevent Depression.

I want more and more people to know and recognize signs of Depression in their loved ones. I was helped by my partner. I came out of it. This is my attempt to pay back life by spreading awareness so that people can reach out to the ones in need. The ones who would never speak or ask for help are the ones who need help more than we realize.

Reviews:

Ruby Drops is a 92 pages long book, and it talks about how the author fought back depression, a 'monster' which if not defeated can defeat you. She described how she fought this with a laser like focus in just forty-five poems which are filled with emotions and pain. Hats off to the author for choosing this topic, because although it's one of the most dangerous mental disease, people talk about it too less and most of the things, it goes neglected or termed as simply 'sadness'. I request everyone to read this book as all of us, at one point of time, get depressed and this book will teach you how to overcome it. – **Kusumita**

Tears are the constant companions in our joinery of life, when we are happy, we simple with a tear drop and when we are sad we are consoled by our running tears. In short life is a rainbow of smiles and tears, these emotions of life are expressed poetically in this book called Ruby Drops by Naseha Sameen. I enjoyed reading (or floating) in this breeze of felonious and emotions, but these one's will stay close to my heart - I Opt for the Curse, Wishing on a Falling Star, Bleeding Heart, My Canvass (very heart touching), Afraid Heart (was this poem written for me...), Unquenched Thirst, Undead Dead, Faraway Place, The Scream and When Moments Live. – **Shunya**

Forty-five heartfelt poems, a great effort. Delicate and poignant paeans to getting in and out of life's dark cul-de-sacs and winning. I liked "Fallen" with its 'ears filled with hollow smiles and laughter' and "Protectors" 'in garb of truth the seller of rosy dreams showered me in the torrent of lies' 'no will to live afraid to die'. – **Flying Painter**

https://www.amazon.in/gp/product/B0184OX190/

Perplex-city

A hustling Millennium city, Gurgoan or rather Gurugram is alive. It lives and breathes like a complex organism. The city has its own though process, its own way of life that is similar to any cosmopolitan and yet very different from the rest. Sharing its borders with New Delhi, Gurgaon stays connected yet aloof.

The city or rather people who made it their home, thrives on its speed and a razor-sharp focus to pick up the pieces and carry on. Not surprising, only thrice in the living history did this city stop to take a breath. And what years where those! The Year of a Rat, the Year of a Pig, and the Year of a Red Snake! For few days in these three years, the city took a pause. However as perplex the psyche of this city, this city did not take a pause like the other cities did.

Perplex-city is a novel that shows intrinsic layer city in its three different lockdowns in three astounding years. The first part is the year of a Rat, a lockdown due to pandemic of COVID-19. The second part is the year of a Pig, when during the communal riots of 1947, the city went in a curfew. And the third part is the year of a Red Snake when due to Sepoy mutiny, in 1857 the city had flag marches and was almost in a lockdown. The events that happened overnight in these strange years!

https://www.amazon.in/gp/product/B09KNVKR9S/

Preview Of Upcoming Novels

Heart of the Ocean

The dark days of poverty, want and overpopulation was far behind. The humanity is now investing in the happiness index and making the world furthermore connected, intuitive and better.

The media is everywhere, people connected to each individual through the high-speed social channel streaming live 24/7. Games, legislatures, rare cop chase, celebrity watch, random shoot that common people upload, the animal rescue, everything was LIVE feed and shared on the large than life digital billboards with people voting "Yeah", "Nay", and commenting. This was the most integral part of life.

One just had to whisper in mind the content and the content stream would be modified. Even if 6 people are standing and staring at the billboard, the content that they see would be different as per the choice made. AI integrated with the master feed and the dermal impact would select and filter the content required in front of the eye.

With resources aplenty, time was given to growth in technology. A decade ago, a scientist chanced upon Cosmic Strip making Time travel a reality. In 10 years, a time council was created Time Council was responsible to maintaining the framework and governance regarding time travel. The Time Council explained the parallel universe When the time traveler kills their grandfather, the traveler is actually killing a parallel universe version of the grandfather, and the time traveler's original universe is unaltered; it has been argued that since the traveler arrives in a different universe's history and not their own history, this is not "genuine" time travel.

The fact that one could never change one's own timeline created a bit of disappointment in public initially. But still Time Council made it their mission to organize picnic and historical tours to past for sake of learning. They along with Time Cops were responsible for the adherence to framework. They had to stop any time smugglers or unauthorized time travelers who would time travel.

Since last 4 years, Time Council hosts "a better ending" annual show. A concept modified from the "Right the Wrong" movement which resulted in the genocide and categorical elimination of race or races in which is now referred as the darkest period of Indian history.

The Time Council came under heavy criticism for adopting a concept that had cause such a genocide. Then Time Council argued that the history had taught, and the lesson was learnt, what better way to remind ourselves of the mistakes than to use the concept for something nobler and bigger than us. They wanted to save lives and correct those unfortunate accidents that were totally avoidable. Not surprisingly few of the of the ethics group were debating on the right of humans to tamper the lives of people from past for their fun.

This year the Time Council decided to integrate fiction into reality, infuse the real events with few of the fictional characters from classic movies to make the events more entertaining. The fictional characters would be the people who were given second chance to life, criminals with implanted memories and cover stories displaced from present to the past. The Time Council as usual would send 2 actors to help save the disaster. This year the better ending event selected to avoid was Titanic disaster. As the events start, number changes happen in the format, to keep up with the pace of the social media. Emma and Aian are sent to save the ship from iceberg. Little did they know that there was terrorist 'The Twins' that had planned to sabotage their efforts to ensure that RMS Titanic sinks on 15th April 1912.

Is life on Titanic different than what it was? How will Emma and Aian ensure that events turn as per the verdict of social media? Will they be able to accomplish their mission? How will the Twins change the course of history? Will Aibak save his actors from the threat of the Twins? Will Reena make the best of the situation and save the Time Council?

Just do not read the novel. This is an interactive novel, where you, as a reader can steer the story to the twists of your choice.

Releasing soon

About the Author

Naseha Sameen

Naseha, a data scientist by profession, is an emerging writer residing in Hyderabad. Her journey as an Author started in 2020 with Invincible Publishers picking up her two books, Heir – End of Innocence & Heir – Dawn of Deception. Set in medieval India, Heir duology is a political thriller. The Lab Academia picked up her 3rd book Perplex-city. For the Thriller lover, Perplex-city is a bouquet of suspense, crime & horror thrillers woven into one novel, where the events of 3 nights change lives & dwarfed the historical events that swept the nation. Her books have been received well for her style and presentation. She has 10 nation-level awards for her books. She has also penned an anthology of poems, Ruby Drops, and co-authored several anthologies. She also co-authored her non-fiction motivational book, TGV Inspiring Lives, and the interactive online novel Cross-Strings.

www.ingramcontent.com/pod-product-compliance
Lightning Source LLC
LaVergne TN
LVHW091636070526
838199LV00044B/1085